THE LOS

The Misfit

A Novel for Teenagers

by

Michael Hambling

Other works by Michael Hambling

The Misfits Series
The Misfits Book 2: The Missing Pilot
The Misfits Book 3: The Poisoned Meadow (out soon)

The Detective Sophie Allen Series
Michael Hambling is the author of the Detective Sophie Allen murder mysteries, all published by Joffe Books. They are also set in Dorset but are written for an adult readership.

Dark Crimes
Deadly Crimes
Secret Crimes
Buried Crimes
Twisted Crimes
Evil Crimes
Shadow Crimes
Silent Crimes
Ruthless Crimes
Brutal Crimes
Hidden Crimes

Visit my website for more news:
www.michaelhambling.co.uk
You can email me at:
michael@michaelhambling.co.uk

Dedication

To my grandchildren: Will, Thomas, Lotty, Daniel, Ben and Esme.

Main characters in this story

The Misfits:
Lee Gibson (15)
Fatima Haddad (16)
Kerry Fenners (17)
Rowan Russell (17)
Danny Fenners (14)
Wolfie Mueller (14)
Josh Kotei   (15)

Several of the characters in this novel made their first appearance in the seventh Sophie Allen novel, Shadow Crimes. It was partly set in Weymouth.

The word tramp has a different meaning in the UK compared to the US. In Britain, a tramp is just an outcast, a homeless person who sleeps rough in the countryside. A tramp might sleep in a disused hut in the woods or somewhere similar.

Chapter 1: An Assembly with a Difference

There he was, up on stage, just about to sit down after speaking. Leroy Saint. Premiership football star. Idol to thousands of fans. And recently come out as gay and proud. He was an icon, adored by his devotees up and down the country, even abroad. There was even a rumour that he'd been offered a role in a big budget film because of his charisma and sleek good looks.

Lee Gibson, sitting in the middle seat of the middle row within the Year 11 block, clapped furiously but suddenly remembered where he was, who he was and who was likely to be watching him. He slowed his applause and nervously looked around. Sure enough, class bully Blagger Banks was looking his way. Had he been spotted? He slowed his handclaps even more and let them die away at the same rate as everyone else. He simply couldn't *not* clap. Not when Leroy had given such an inspirational talk on human rights and LGBT inclusion. It was everything Lee believed in. The trouble was, Blagger Banks and his two thuggish pals didn't believe in it and let everyone else in the class know exactly what they thought about LGBT rights.

Lee glanced round again, and his stomach felt as if it was turning to water. Blagger wasn't applauding. He was staring at Lee, a smirk on his face. He must have spotted Lee's enthusiastic reaction to the talk. His look said it all. *You gay weirdo. I'm gonna get you after school. Again.*

Why did people like Blagger even exist? What use were they to the human race, with their constant bullying of anyone who was different in some way, however slight? Lee wished he had superpowers that would let him floor Blagger with one gigantic blow and protect peaceful people for ever. The harsh reality was that Lee was a thin lightweight who didn't stand a chance against the tall, heavily built Blagger. Added to which, he didn't even know anyone else in the school who felt like he did. He knew other gay people existed. There was Leroy Saint up on stage, just sitting down after saying he was gay and proud, and being thanked by Mr McNultie, the headteacher, for being such a good role model. But it was different for grown-ups. They had jobs and earned money. They had power and influence. And they didn't have people like Blagger Banks to deal with every single school-day.

Lee wondered if there was a way he could somehow avoid the trio on his way home but suspected they'd be lurking at the entrance and would ambush him whichever way he went. They knew where he lived. Could he hide in the building for half an hour or so until they got fed up and cleared off? It might be worth a try.

The school day turned out to be worse than he'd feared. Blagger lost no opportunity to taunt Lee with insults. *Gay worm. Girlie boy. Shitfaced poof.* His two mates just stood grinning and bunching their fists.

At the end of the afternoon Lee slid along to his form room and asked Mrs Norman, his form tutor, if she needed any help. She said thanks but she had a meeting to go to. He tried the art room, but an art club had

6

already started setting up. He couldn't join the club because he was crap at art, and he knew how good they all were. They had stuff exhibited in the town hall. He was wandering along the corridor wondering where he could go when he nearly bumped into Guy Grainger, the assistant caretaker, transferring boxes into a cupboard. Guy was old and had a limp, but he was always friendly.

'Hi, Guy,' Lee said. 'Do you want a hand?'

Guy slid his glasses back up his nose and peered out of the cupboard to see who'd spoken. He smiled. 'Oh yeah. A big strong lad like you. Just what I need.' He laughed.

Lee, who was short and thin, must have looked dejected because Guy patted him on the shoulder. 'Yeah, come on. Any help is good help.'

Lee's mood lifted during the next twenty minutes as he chatted aimlessly to Guy while stacking boxes. He checked the time when the job was finished. A clear half-hour had passed since the bell had rung for the end of lessons. Surely he'd be safe by now? He left Guy and walked towards the entrance, peering outside. There was hardly anybody in sight, not even the thuggish Blagger and his pals. Lee slipped out of the door and made his way carefully down the drive to the main gate. Once outside he stayed close to the hedge, hoping his grey uniform clothes would blend into the dark colours of the evergreen shrubs. What kind of a life was this? Other people from his class could walk down the street noisily, swinging their bags and larking about, laughing and joking. Whereas he had to be on constant alert, peering around corners, scanning the entrances to

7

shops and cafes, checking the people standing in a bus queue. It was all too much. He wondered how much more of this he could take. And all this on the very same day that Leroy Saint had spoken up for gay rights at his school assembly.

He turned into a side road. Not far to go. Over the railway bridge with its view of the nearby nature reserve, around the corner, down the avenue and he'd be home. Maybe he'd been worrying needlessly. He stood on the bridge to watch a train go under, then quickened his step as he rounded the corner. He nearly cannoned into the stocky body of Blagger Banks. The two flunkies stepped in behind Lee. He was trapped.

'Worm,' Blagger said. 'Slug. Gay shitface. Thought you'd avoid us, did you? No chance. I'm not stupid and I hate poofs.'

Lee remained silent. After all, what was there to say that he hadn't already tried on all the previous occasions he'd been ambushed like this? He'd be punched a few times, maybe kicked. They'd push him down onto the ground and spit in his face. They'd laugh at him, give him a final kick then slowly wander off in search of other entertainment. That was the usual sequence. He tensed himself. Where would the first punch land? It caught him out though, that first touch. It wasn't a punch at all. It was a hard kick on the shins that caused him to double up in pain.

'Oi! I saw that. Leave him alone.' Two girls on the other side of the street came running across. They were in jeans and trainers, and carried shoulder bags. Sixth formers from the local college.

8

Blagger turned and sneered at them. 'Piss off. What's it got to do with you? Who are you anyway?' He grabbed a handful of Lee's hair and tugged him forward.

'Kerry Fenners,' the shorter, sharp-faced one replied. 'And I told you to leave him alone.'

Blagger looked blankly at her. One of his buddies suddenly looked worried and put a hand on Blagger's shoulder as if to warn him but he ignored it.

'And I told you to piss off,' he said, letting go of Lee and trying to shove Kerry away. What happened next was a blur. A fist caught him in the chest, causing him to double up. Another followed like a flash, this time into his face.

'Do you think I'm scared of a fat slug like you?' she hissed. 'This is Lee Gibson and he's a friend of my brother's. You ever touch him again and I'll come after you. And you won't ever forget it. Understand?' She squared up to Blagger and grabbed his bleeding nose, pulling it hard. 'I said, have you got that?'

Blagger nodded, sniffling. The two acolytes backed away, hauling Blagger with them.

'You don't wanna mess with her,' one of them said to Blagger. 'She's mad. Total. She jumps through shop windows just for the fun of it.'

They hurried around the corner, the sound of their footsteps quickly fading.

Kerry looked at Lee and frowned. 'Why don't you stand up to them? If you just put up with it, it just gets worse. That's what bullies are like.'

Lee rubbed his leg. 'I did the first time. Tried to fight back. But that made them all join in. It's never been as

9

bad since. I just switch off and let it happen. They give up sooner. Thanks for what you did. Do I really know your brother?'

'Danny. He doesn't go to your school, but he plays sax in the area youth band, like you.'

Realisation hit Lee. 'Oh, you're that Kerry. I've heard of you.'

'Yeah, well. I used to be famous around the town.'

'You mean notorious,' the other girl broke in, laughing. She was taller than Kerry and had a deeper voice. 'I'd even heard of you, from my sheltered background. The mad Kerry Fenners. That violent, drunken slut. Someone to avoid.'

Kerry pushed her mousey-coloured fringe back from her forehead and grinned back. 'Didn't you know? That's all well in the past. I'm a reformed character now. That's what I told the cops, anyway. But my old reputation does come in useful sometimes.'

The taller girl turned to Lee. 'I'm Rowan and Kerry's my best friend. At least I like to think so. We overheard what that idiot was saying. Are you gay?'

Lee wasn't sure how to respond. Maybe these two girls deserved honesty after saving him from Blagger. 'I think so. I'm a bit confused really.'

'Aren't we all. I'm trans, by the way, if it makes you feel any easier. I've only been a girl for six months. Kerry might act tough, but she's been the best friend I've ever had. We've only known each other since September when we started at college.'

By now Lee had got his breath back. Was this the time to finally open up to someone? 'I've never really

10

talked to anyone about it, about how I feel. I'm scared about it. I just know I'm different to what people expect. I mean, I really like girls but not in that way. I can't even make sense of it myself.'

Rowan was nodding. 'Yeah, that's it. That's what the normals don't understand. They think we've chosen it somehow. They think we must understand it. But we haven't and we don't. It's just the way we are.' She stopped and looked at Lee carefully. 'Listen. We've got the option of using a room in the local community centre for an evening each week, for free. Kerry's granddad's a part-time caretaker there. We've been thinking of starting a group up. Do you want to come along? It'll be cool.'

Lee couldn't hide his enthusiasm. 'A sort of LGBT group for teens? Yeah, totally. What night?'

Kerry took over. 'Mondays. But we don't want everyone to know, so keep it quiet. I don't want any trouble 'cos Gramps isn't up to dealing with it, so it'll only be people we trust. And it won't be just LGBT. It's for anyone who feels left out. I'll be there and so will Danny. We go with Gramps anyway. Danny's got Asperger's. Did you know?'

Lee looked puzzled. 'What's that?'

'He's kind of awkward a lot of the time. He doesn't chat much and gets tense around other people. Haven't you guessed? I thought you were friends.'

Lee shrugged. 'We only chat a bit. Tell jokes. We try out tunes together when we have a break. He's nice.'

Kerry smiled. 'Listen, if you think he's nice then that makes us friends. Okay? He's my kid brother and I look after him. Well, me and Gramps.'

Lee wondered whether to ask why Kerry's mum and dad didn't look after them but decided not to. Better not pry. He realised that Rowan was checking the time on her phone.

'We'd better be off,' she said. 'Homework to do early. Kerry and I are off into town tonight.'

'Boyfriend hunting,' Kerry laughed. 'I'm teaching her the ropes. She's a total beginner. Can you believe it with her looks?'

The two girls hurried away giggling. Lee felt a hundred times better than he had for months. Maybe he'd write an appreciation of Leroy Saint's talk and submit it for the next school magazine. The deadline was still a couple of weeks away.

Chapter 2: Making Plans

The next day was Friday and Lee felt nervous. Not only would he be meeting Blagger in registration, but this was followed by double English, the only subject in which they were in the same set. He needn't have worried. Blagger kept his head down and hardly spoke. Several other classmates noted his black eye and felt confident enough to try some gentle teasing. Blagger merely scowled at them. Lee, wisely, didn't join in.

He thought that Kerry Fenners was an interesting enough character to warrant some research. How to go about it? He asked his English teacher at the end of the lesson but changed the details, telling her that his research was about a local teenage music and sports enthusiast.

'Well, if she's well-known locally, there may be something about her in the Gazette. It has a website so start there. They often carry stories of local concerts by bands and orchestras and often name soloists. And you say she also plays sports? The Gazette will be your best bet for that as well. So can we expect something in this term's magazine from you, Lee?'

'Maybe,' he replied. 'But not this. I was thinking of doing something on Leroy Saint's talk. What do you think, Miss?'

'That's a really good idea. If you decide to go ahead, remember what I taught you. List your sources. But you ought to speak to Fatima first. She's already planning something like that. Maybe you could do a joint effort.'

Lee frowned. 'Who?'

'Fatima Haddad. She started here about two years ago, when you were in year nine. She's one of the refugees from Syria. She's the editor, Lee, and is on the school council. Surely you've spotted her name somewhere around? She's a real highflier. She's in 11B.'

'Okay, I'll find her. Thanks, Miss.'

He hurried away, feeling stupid. He knew what the problem was. He'd been so bound up in his own troubles during the past year that he'd ignored everything else. He existed in a bubble. He now needed to make up for lost time. He headed for 11B's form room and looked around for someone he knew. There was Marty Penning, in the same science set as Lee and always friendly.

'Hi, Marty. I'm looking for someone called Fatima? She runs the school mag?'

Marty rolled his eyes melodramatically. 'Well, Fatima runs everything. She's over there in the corner, brushing her hair. Good luck. Hope you escape with your life.'

Lee looked across just as Fatima glanced up. She was olive skinned, with shiny black hair pulled into a tight ponytail. She gave him a smile, so he walked across. He felt nervous, as always, but he held Kerry Fenners' confident manner in mind. He could do this.

'Hi. I'm Lee. Miss Hunt, my English teacher, said you were writing an article about Leroy Saint's talk. Can I help?'

When she spoke, her voice had a definite inflexion and she seemed to pick her words carefully. 'Oh, wow. Of course. I only said I'd do it 'cause I didn't think anyone else would. You can do it all if you like.'

14

'I don't think I'm that good. I've never done anything for the mag before. For any mag.'

She smiled. 'You just gotta go for it. But I can help if you like. I've put some ideas down on paper. Look, why don't you summarise his talk and I'll do a commentary? About a thousand words in total. That should be about right. Keep it sharp.'

Lee wondered if he was up to the task. 'You sound as if you know what you're talking about,' he said.

'My father was a newspaper editor back in Syria,' she said quietly. 'Though he went to university in London when he was younger.'

Lee failed to pick up on the sadness in her voice. 'What does he do now?' he asked.

She turned away. 'I've got to go. Look, if you want to talk a bit more about the article, we could meet for a few minutes at home time. I'll see you outside.'

She picked up her bag rather abruptly and walked out. Marty Penning waited for Lee at the door. It was double science next, so they walked along the corridor together.

'Did you find out what you wanted?' Marty asked.

'Sort of. But she went out in a hurry. I may have said something to upset her.'

'Easy to do. She comes from Syria. She clams up when anyone asks about it.'

Year 11 were first for dinners on Fridays, so Lee had the rest of the lunch break to do some checking in the library. He was one of the first into lunch and one of the first to leave. He had quite a list of things to research, so he didn't want to waste any time.

It was easy to find information about Leroy Saint. The footballer even had his own website with links to his campaign work. The article would be easier than Lee had thought, especially if his contribution was to be the factual part. He made some notes so that he could work on the story at home during the weekend, if he could find the time. He stared at the screen. Who was he kidding? What else would he be doing? His life wasn't exactly a non-stop, social merry-go-round, even at weekends.

He moved on to Kerry Fenners, looking for her name in local newspaper articles. It cropped up several times but not in association with any reports about anti-social behaviour. His eyes widened when he read the story of the house fire that had killed her parents. So that's why she and Danny lived with their grandfather. But why were there no accounts of the anti-social behaviour that Rowan had mentioned the day before? He went across to speak to Mrs Hall, the librarian.

'If the person was a teenager, Lee, their names couldn't be published in the press for minor crimes and petty vandalism, even if the police were involved. Everyone deserves the chance to change as they grow up. Don't you agree? Anyway, wouldn't it be a bit like stalking if you really started looking for information about other people? That is, unless they're famous. You don't really want to do that, do you?'

He reluctantly agreed and returned to his seat. Maybe she was right. Maybe he shouldn't be looking for information about people's pasts. There was one more, though, before he stopped. Fatima Haddad.

He read the news account open-mouthed. Fatima's father was dead, killed by an artillery shell deliberately aimed at their house in Syria. Her younger sister had been killed too. Her mother, younger brother and Fatima herself escaped because they were out at the time. They were smuggled out of the country with a death threat hanging over them. Fatima's mother was a doctor and now worked at the local medical centre here in Weymouth. She'd sometimes spoken out against the bombing in Syria, even on British TV. No wonder Fatima seemed so self-assured but sad. And he thought he had troubles. Get real, Lee, he said to himself.

The final afternoon bell was followed by the usual stampede towards the exits. Lee took his time, strolled outside and waited on one side of the path. He didn't have long to wait before Fatima appeared. She looked surprised to see him.

'I thought you wouldn't bother,' she said. 'I've lost count of the number of people who say they're going to write something, then I never hear from them again.'

'No, I will write something,' he replied. 'I've already got the background. I did it in the library at lunchtime. Mrs Hall helped me.'

'That's good. We can chat while we walk,' she said. 'I live on the estate next to yours.'

'Don't you get a bus?' Lee asked as they headed away from the school. 'A lot of the people who live further out than me do.'

She shook her head. 'We can't afford it. I walk to save money.'

He was puzzled. 'Isn't your mum a doctor? Don't they earn a lot?'

She stared at him. 'How did you know that?'

Lee thought quickly. 'I think she treated my Mum once.'

Fatima seemed to accept this hasty explanation. 'We send money back to my uncle's family. They're still trapped in Syria and survive on whatever they can. My mum's also putting money aside for my brother and me, for when we go to university. It's hard.'

Lee didn't know what to say. Hardly anyone he knew was making plans for that far ahead. He decided to change the subject and started to talk about the article. Fatima seemed impressed by his ideas. Within a few minutes they'd decided on the content and Fatima sketched out a plan in her notebook. She tore the page out and passed it over.

'Why do you want to write about him?'

Lee felt his cheeks burning. 'He's a hero of mine,' he mumbled.

Her dark eyes seemed to burn into him. 'Why? Do you think you might be gay?'

He didn't answer. He just stood there, blushing furiously, not knowing what to say.

'I don't really know what I am,' she said. 'I'm sort of interested in boys, but I like girls as well. I mean, I might be attracted to them a bit, as well. It's all so tricky, isn't it? Does that mean I might be bi? I wish I knew. At the moment I've just got friends, and I wonder a bit about all the other stuff. It's all new to me. It's not something we ever talk about much. That's a shame, I think.' She gave him a mischievous smile. She was so different now she was out of the school buildings, though he was still a bit in awe of her. He didn't yet have as clear a picture of himself as she did of the person she really was. Maybe it was all the trauma she'd been through. It would probably cause someone to stop and take stock.

'I think I might be gay but it's all so confusing. I don't like all the rough stuff that some boys get up to and I like the company of girls more. But I don't think stuff like that means people are gay. I think it's different. It's just who you fancy. Some really tough men are gay, football and rugby players, and soldiers in the army.' He paused. 'I haven't told anyone this kinda stuff before. And I've never got involved with anyone, not yet.' He suddenly stopped. 'Listen, I found out yesterday about a sort of youth minorities and LGBT group that might be starting up in town on Monday evening in the Community Centre. Interested?'

She smiled again. 'Oh, yes.'

Chapter 3: The Misfits Meet

Lee and Fatima had arranged to meet outside the Community Centre at seven thirty. He hardly recognised her out of her school uniform. She looked older and more mature, helped by the skinny jeans and leather jacket she was wearing. Her eyes were lined with a purple eyeshadow.

'You look really cool,' he said.

'I thought you weren't interested in girls,' she laughed.

'I'm not really. But I like colour. See, I've got a red shirt on.' He unzipped his hoodie so she could see.

'Very fash,' she commented. 'Not sure who'll be here to impress, though. I thought you said it was two other girls?'

'Yeah, Kerry and Rowan. But they might've invited a few other people. I saw Danny at jazz band practise on Saturday morning and told him you'd be coming. He's Kerry's brother and he said he'd be here. He didn't know who else would be. Let's go in.'

The centre was an old, redbrick building but at least it was warm, even in the lobby. Their footsteps must have sounded because Kerry appeared at a doorway along the corridor.

'We're in here,' she said. 'Though there's only me, Danny and Rowan so far. A couple of other people have messaged to say they'll come but they're not here yet. You must be Fatima.'

The Syrian girl gave a cautious smile. 'Yeah. I hope you don't mind. Lee told me about your idea. I think it's great.'

They followed Kerry into a small meeting room, set with soft chairs. A plate of chocolate biscuits was on a small table in the middle.

'Who else are you expecting?' Fatima asked.

The reply came from Rowan. 'We put some posters up in the common room at college. Maybe one of two more? I'm Rowan, by the way. You're Fatima? I've heard of you, even before this was arranged. You're into campaigns, like me. I think I saw you at the environment march back in the spring.'

'Yeah, I was there. Great, wasn't it? I wrote an article about it for our school mag. That's how I got landed with being the editor.'

Lee's head was buzzing. He felt a real thrill at being among a small group of people who probably shared his sense of being an outsider, ill at ease in most situations. In here he felt as if he belonged, for the first time in several years. He joined Danny, Kerry's younger brother, in munching through several chocolate biscuits. They chatted about their saxophones and the music they'd been rehearsing at Saturday's band practice. They both looked up as several figures appeared at the door.

'Is this the new group?' A grey-haired man pushed a wheelchair into the room. 'We bumped into the caretaker, and he told us you'd be along here.'

'Okay, Dad. I can take it from here,' said the boy in the wheelchair. He had a shock of blonde hair and lots of freckles. Once his father had left, he grinned madly and spoke at top speed. 'I'm Wolfie. Wolfie Mueller. I heard about you from my older brother at college. He said there was a new support group for minorities, and I am absolutely part of a minority. I want to get involved. Whatever it is, whatever we're doing, count me in. Totally. Think what you'll be missing if you don't let me join. All my talent, all my good looks, all my buzz. All going to waste. You need me. You really do. I'm guaranteed to bring a smile to anyone's face. I know all the best jokes, and I don't bite. Come on. You know you want to.' He brought his wheelchair into the middle of the room at top speed and skidded to a stop, looking around. 'Come on, guys. Wakey, wakey.'

Kerry spoke up. 'Course you can join. I s'pose Rowan and me are in charge at the mo, until we get something sorted. We was thinking we'd wait ten minutes or so, then we'd say a bit about ourselves. Sort of break the ice. Is that okay?'

Rowan looked at the clock on the wall. 'That's ten mins now. Why don't we start? Let's all sit down. I'll go first, then everyone talks in turn in a circle like, and we finish with Kerry.' She watched as the others agreed enthusiastically. 'Okay, so I'm Rowan Russell. I'm seventeen and I'm trans. I'm at college doing health and social care. I was a boy until last year but now I'm a girl and I'm really, really happy about it. I'm so happy about it that I can't describe it. I want to keep jumping up and down in happiness. That's how it feels to me. I want to be a nurse when I'm older. That means going to uni, and that might be tough. But nothing is as tough as the way

I felt for the last couple of years.' She turned to Danny and indicated that he should take over.

'I'm Danny Fenners, I'm fourteen and I've got Asperger's. I get stressed around other people. I always want things to be right and start to feel funny if they aren't. Kerry and me live with Gramps 'cos our parents died in a fire last year. It's really cool 'cos Gramps is good fun and treats us like grown-ups. We have a real laugh. Kerry and Rowan said I could come along 'cos this group wasn't just for LGBT stuff. I play saxophone and that's how I met Lee. I want to be a scientist when I grow up.'

Danny, the youngest person there, had looked petrified as he spoke, but he relaxed as he finished. Everyone clapped because he looked so relieved.

Rowan smiled at him. 'Thanks, Danny. That was really good. Remember this group isn't just for LGBT. It's for anyone who feels left out. We're just a group of friends meeting up in a safe space. It's you next, Lee.'

Lee swallowed his last mouthful of biscuit and started to speak. He was interrupted though by the sight of a boy's face peering around the door. He was black and smiled nervously at the small group. 'My big sister saw your poster and told me about it. I'm Josh. Can I come in?'

'Of course,' Rowan said. 'We've only just started. Sit down. I'm Rowan, and Danny here has just finished telling us about himself. Lee's next.'

Josh stepped quietly into the room and sat down. He was tall and slim but looked wary.

Lee was nervous when he started speaking. 'Well, I'm a bit unsure about what I am. All I know is, it's different from most of my classmates. The ones who are boys, I mean. Not much of what they say makes sense to me, not the stuff they say about girls. I don't know what to think about how I feel, but I know it's different. I can't say much else, but I'm glad to be here. Is that okay?' He looked across at Rowan.

'Yeah, of course,' she replied. 'And don't worry about being unsure about yourself. You gotta give it time. Who's next?'

Fatima started speaking, picking her words carefully, something Lee had begun to get used to. 'I'm Fatima Haddad. I'm from Syria. My father was a journalist opposed to the regime. He was killed, with my younger sister, during shelling that blew our house up. I escaped with my mother and my brother, but we were chased. We've been in Britain for nearly three years. My mother is a doctor. I want to study law and politics and go back to Syria when the war ends and help mend my country. I might be gay but I might not be. My mother doesn't know, and I don't know how to tell her. I'm so sad because otherwise we're really close. I stay busy to stop myself thinking about it. It's so good that I've met you all.'

There was silence when Fatima stopped speaking. She dropped her eyes and stared at the floor. Rowan started clapping and the rest quickly followed but Fatima didn't look up. Lee thought she looked sadder than anyone he'd ever seen but then she seemed to

24

gather herself together, looked up at the others and smiled.

'Got to keep on going,' she said. 'I'm doing it for my dad.'

'Wow,' Wolfie said. 'That is so awesome. You're a hero, Fatima. Anyway, I'm Wolfie Mueller. My real name is Wolfgang and Dad is from Germany. Mum's English, though. I've been like this since I was small, in a wheelchair. I've got a problem with my spine and get treated in hospital two or three times a year. But there might be some more treatment coming so I'm hopeful that I might be able to walk sometime in the future. There are loads of people worse off than me though. I've been looking for something like this for ages, coming to a group of dudes who feel a bit different, like me. It's brilliant. I'm fourteen, like Danny. I like chicken burgers and pizza. Shall I tell you a joke? What did the hot dog say when his friend passed him in the running race? Wow, I relish the fact that you've mustard the strength to ketchup to me.'

Rowan waited until the laughter subsided. 'Great, Wolfie. That's impressive. Who's next? I think it's probably you.' She looked at the newcomer. 'Don't be nervous. We're all friends here.'

'I'm not normally nervous like this. I passed by a homeless person just out there at the back of the centre and some drunk idiots were having a go at her. I told them to leave her alone. They backed off but gave me the finger. I hope she's alright.'

Rowan frowned. 'Maybe we should go and check on her. Where was it? We didn't see anyone when we arrived.'

Josh scratched his head. 'It was down the side road. I live over the back a few streets away. And yeah, I think we should see if she's okay. Maybe take her a couple of biscuits?'

The group hurried out of the room and Kerry had a few words with her grandfather. 'We'll be back really quick,' she told him.

Chapter 4: Meeting the Outcast

The teenagers went outside and made their way down the quiet side road that Josh had described. They could see a small knot of figures ahead of them. It looked as though they were clustered around the doorway of a disused shop.

'They've come back,' Josh said. 'Well, two of them. There were three earlier.'

The two people blocking the doorway, both teenagers, stepped back and looked up as they heard approaching footsteps.

'She's still there,' Josh added. 'Look. What have they done?'

A grubby-faced woman could be seen peering out from under a soiled duvet. She had smears of blood on her face, mixed with tears. She tried to wipe her face with a hand but only succeeded in spreading the streak of blood further across her cheek. Her nose was bleeding.

Kerry rounded on the duo. You bastards,' she hissed at them. 'You slimy bullies. Is that what you do? Pick on people who can't fight back? That's so shitty. Why don't you all piss off and leave her alone?' She stopped and looked at the girl who was hanging back behind the other one. 'I know you from somewhere.'

The duo turned tail and hurried off. Meanwhile Rowan and Josh were checking on the woman, helping her to clean her face with some tissues. Fatima had grabbed a couple of biscuits from the plate on her way out of the community centre and gave them to the victim, now looking a little better, though still wary. She took a swig of water from a bottle that Rowan offered her. They finally managed to glean some information from the woman. Her name was Daisy and she'd been sleeping rough for the last few weeks after being evicted from her small home. It was difficult to follow all that she said but it seemed that she'd lost her job and had no money. She told them that the girl had suddenly kicked her in the face without warning. It had taken her by surprise.

'Do you want some soup?' Kerry asked. 'There was a tin of veggie stuff back in the centre. It'll only take me five minutes to heat it up and bring it in a mug.'

She and Fatima set off back to the centre, leaving the other five with the outcast. Lee felt ill at ease. He kept looking across the road at the small green opposite. It was deep in shadow with small clumps of trees and bushes. He felt they were being watched. He turned to Josh.

'Is there someone across there, spying on us?'

Josh peered across into the gloomy darkness. He shook his head. 'I can't tell. But there was an older person with those two earlier on. I reckon he's put them up to it. He might be across there. Maybe we should go across to see.'

Rowan was making sure that the tramp-woman was okay. She'd finished wiping the dirt and blood smeared face. They'd all thought she was old when they first saw her because her skin was so grimy that it looked lined. But now, cleaned up, they realised that she was only in her thirties, although she looked pale and ill.

28

'Do you need to see a doctor, Daisy?' Rowan asked.

The woman shook her head. 'Nah. I'm okay, honest. And they'd want me to fill in forms and sign things. I ain't doin' any of that stuff.'

It wasn't long before Kerry and Fatima came back, each carrying a mug of steaming soup. While Daisy was sipping it, Lee and Josh slipped across the road and entered the grassy area, trying to peer through the gloom. They stood for a while then returned to the group clustered around Daisy.

'We think someone was across there watching,' Lee said. 'Something or someone jumped over the fence at the back when we got close.'

'What's on the other side of the fence?' Wolfie asked. 'Is it someone's garden?'

Kerry shook her head. 'It's a path that takes you into the estate. Did you get a look at this other person, Josh? When you passed earlier?'

He shook his head. 'Not really. Whoever it was, he was hanging back from the other two, just watching. He was a bit bigger than the others. But they kept glancing round as if they were checking with him. He just nodded. But I couldn't see clearly 'cos he had his hood up. That's if it was a he. It could've been a woman.'

Rowan looked again at the outcast. 'Daisy, we gotta get back to the centre. Are you sure you'll be alright here?'

Daisy was already looking better after finishing one of the mugs of soup. 'Yeah. I've been kipping here all week and that was the first bit o' trouble. Don't you go worrying about me.'

'Well, some of us'll check up on you from time to time. Alright? Maybe bring you some food?'

Daisy smiled for the first time, revealing a gap in her front teeth. 'Yeah, but not cheese. I can't stand cheese. Makes me fart summat rotten.'

The group laughed.

'Can't have that, polluting the air,' Wolfie said. They laughed even more.

'You look like a real gang of misfits, but thanks,' Daisy said when she finished the soup. The group drifted back to the community centre.

'That was really good, Josh,' Rowan said as they each took another biscuit and sat down. 'You could've ignored it and not told us. Then she might have got a real kicking. You did the right thing. Now tell us a bit about yourself.'

Josh shrugged. 'Not much to tell, really. My names Josh Kotei and I'm fifteen. Dad says I'm too quiet, Mum says I'm too noisy. One teacher says I've got real potential, but another says I don't work hard enough. I don't know where I am, really. I like taking photos. I've got two cameras, but I got them second hand. I want to be a photographer when I'm older. I need some quality kit first, though. And probably some qualifications. Oh, and as you've spotted, I'm black. Both my parents come from London. I just wanna get on with my life but somehow I don't fit in, not even with other black guys. Dunno what the problem is, though. It's all a bit weird.'

Rowan thanked him. 'That's cool, Josh. You've fitted in already. It's just you now, Kerry. Get ready for fireworks, everyone.'

Kerry gave a big grin. 'Thanks, cheeky-face. This is so cool, meeting like this. It's better than I ever thought it would be. I'm Kerry Fenners, Danny's sister. I'm seventeen and best friends with Rowan. I'm not gay or trans or anything like that, but I've got anger issues. That's what my counsellor tells me. I used to be really wild. Drunk and a bit of a slut but I'm trying to get over it. You mustn't feel sorry for Danny and me. Danny told you what happened to our mum and dad, but our family life was a mess. It's better now. Gramps is the caretaker here on three evenings a week so found us this room to use, but it's all official. We're not here on the sly. The manager knows. What we've got to do now is decide what we're gonna do. Anyone got ideas?'

There were a few moments of silence. Wolfie spoke first.

'We could do some social things. You know, like bowling.'

'That's a good idea. We'd have to go out for that, though. But it'd be fun. It's given me an idea. Gramps said they have a table tennis table here and an old snooker table. He found them in a back cupboard. We could get them out sometimes. How does that sound?'

Everyone nodded enthusiastically.

'Another thing,' Kerry continued. 'Danny and me, we know a police person. She's a detective and she's trans. We could get her down to talk to us. Tell us what to do if someone has a go at us. What do you think? Her name's Rae and she's good fun.'

'Yeah, I like that idea,' Wolfie replied, enthusiastically. 'Sort of mix up fun stuff with serious stuff. Cool. And we could do things like we've just done. You know, helping that woman. We could call ourselves the Misfits, just like she said. What do the rest of you guys think?'

They all agreed that this was the right approach and a good group name. Kerry looked across at Rowan and grinned. They'd got started!

Chapter 5: Disappearance

The next morning Kerry walked slowly out of the classroom, packing her books away at the end of her first lesson, and found Rowan waiting for her.

'Daisy, the down and out from last night, isn't in that doorway anymore. I walked by this morning and there was no sign of her or any of her stuff.'

'That's a bit weird,' Kerry replied. 'She never said she'd be leaving, did she?'

Rowan shook her head. 'Nope. The way she lay back after finishing the soup made me think she was settled for the night.'

'Could she have left early? What time did you check?'

'I went by on my way here. I took a detour 'cos I had some sandwiches for her. I got my mum to make a couple extra. Do you think we should take a closer look?'

Kerry thought for a few moments. 'Yeah. I usually have lunch here but if you've got spare sandwiches, I could have them instead. So let's go at the start of lunch. Okay?'

'It's a deal.'

As Rowan had said, the doorway was empty with nothing to be seen, not even any litter or residual bits and pieces.

'It looks as though it's been swept,' Kerry said. 'Don't most tramps leave stuff when they move on? They're not usually the tidiest people in the world, are they?'

Despite her reputation for having anger-fuelled confrontations, Kerry was a very tidy person. When her parents were alive, she'd cleaned the house regularly, washed the laundry and done most of the grocery shopping. Her mother had spent most of the time drunk and her father had been a criminal thug. If Kerry hadn't performed these tasks, no one else would, and young Danny's life might have descended into chaos. Now they were both living with their grandfather there was much less need for her meticulous tidiness, but she found it hard to relax and let Gramps do most of the household chores. She picked up the single item of debris, a torn piece of paper that had blown into the corner of the entrance. She examined it on both sides, frowning. It was blank except for the two letters H and E, scribbled faintly in pencil on one side. Rowan peered over her shoulder.

'What do you think it means?' Kerry asked. 'Maybe it's nothing to do with Daisy but just a scrap of paper blown in here by the wind.'

'Could be. But they're the first two letters of help. Do you think those nutters came back for her last night? Didn't Lee say that he thought someone was across the road watching us when we were here? What if they just waited 'til we were gone and then came back for her? Maybe they kicked her around a bit more then took her with them to hide the evidence. What if she's been dumped somewhere where it'll be hard to spot her?'

Kerry looked worried. 'I dunno. Maybe we'd better have a scout around to see if there are any signs. We've got ten minutes before we need to start back.'

34

The two girls checked around the area for several minutes but failed to spot anything that would help them in their quest to find Daisy. They did find some other debris, though, and it worried them.

'Druggies?' Kerry asked as they stood peering into the small play park opposite the abandoned shop doorway.

'Looks like it,' Rowan replied. 'I wouldn't let my kids anywhere near this place if I was a parent. It's gross. Look over there in that corner. I'm not sure it's even dog poo. Do you think the local cops know about it?'

Kerry shrugged. 'Hardly ever see cops around the streets now, anywhere. It's all these cuts, I s'pect. Maybe I ought to give Rae a call today. She's my detective friend. I was gonna wait a few days.'

'Good idea. We need to do something in case Daisy's in trouble,' Rowan said. 'We'd better be getting back.'

Kerry phoned her police contact later that afternoon and had a short chat. Rae said that she'd find out what she could, but that homeless people often went walkabout without any warning. She then offered to pay Kerry a visit the following evening and meet up with any of the other group members who were free.

Kerry sent a text message around to the other Misfit members about an emergency meeting the following evening. Then she met up with Rowan. They decided to pay another visit to the area from where Daisy had vanished, this time to speak to neighbouring shop owners. Maybe one of them had spotted something suspicious.

The two girls started at the doorway of the disused shop, still grubby, with a few bits of litter blowing about in the breeze. A launderette with a *For Sale* sign was next door so they walked in and had a short chat with the manager, a woman who was sweeping the floor half-heartedly.

'That tramp's been in the doorway for the past two weeks,' she said in response to Kerry's question. 'She's not there in the middle of the day, 'cos she goes closer into the town centre to beg. There's no point in beggars trying to put out a collection tin around here. People don't have much spare cash. She'd always be back in that doorway by early evening. I felt sorry for her, but she was a bit of a nuisance. It puts people off coming in when there's a down-and-out with all their stuff spread out just next door. She smelled a bit. I reckon my early evening trade dropped off a bit once she arrived.'

'Is that why you're selling up?' Rowan asked.

'No. I decided to move out more than a month ago. This whole area has gone downhill recently. But her being here didn't help.' The woman turned away as if she didn't want the two girls to see her face.

The owner of the small general store on the other side had similar views. He was stacking shelves when they went in.

'She put people off, sprawled across the doorway like that. My daytime trade didn't change much. That was when she was away somewhere else. But it put local customers off in the mornings and evenings. I felt sorry for her, but when it affects business you can only go so far. I used to give her a few bits and pieces of leftover food, but I stopped doing that when I saw my takings were going down. Something should be done for people like her. We shouldn't be expected to put up with people roughing it in the doorways along here.'

'Did you see anything last night before she disappeared?' Rowan asked.

He shook his head. 'That must have been after I closed. Later in the week I stay open until nine but on Monday nights I shut at seven.'

'Can you think of anyone who might have harmed her? Someone saw her being bullied earlier, before she went missing,' Kerry said.

He turned away to straighten up some cans that already seemed to be perfectly in line. 'No.'

The two girls left the shop and walked across to the small park.

'Do you get the feeling that they know more than they're willing to tell us?' Kerry asked.

'Yeah, definitely. They were both a bit cagey about something. Maybe we should tell your police person tomorrow evening when we see her.' She looked around her at the litter on the ground. 'It's a bit grubby here, isn't it? I mean, when you compare it with other play areas in the town. There's a lot of these small plastic bags around. And just look at all the fag ends and drink cans. I don't like this place much, Kerry.'

Kerry sniffed the air. 'Nor do I. There's something nasty about it. C'mon. Let's go home.'

They didn't spot that they were being watched from behind a clump of bushes.

Chapter 6: Fruit Cake

Wednesday evening was chilly, damp and drizzly. Surely the weather wasn't about to take a severe turn for the worst just as the October half-term holiday started? That would be a real pain. Wolfie Mueller made sure that he listed his homework assignments as soon as he arrived home from school. There might be a week and a half of holiday ahead, but school project work would probably take up several days. He decided to get started on the geography one right away, while it was fresh in his mind. He had a spare hour before dinner. He sure didn't want to miss out on this emergency meeting of the Misfits with the police friend of Kerry's. He'd never had a conversation with a cop before. He tried to steer clear of trouble. He had enough problems in his life without the extra stress that would have built up if he'd got involved in shoplifting with some of his friends. They'd been questioned during some low-level police enquiries. They pinched things from the Saturday morning market stalls and had asked him a couple of times if he'd act as lookout and receiver, smuggling the items away from the market area, hidden in his wheelchair. He'd declined the request as tactfully as he could, explaining that his getaway would be severely impeded compared to their ability to scarper at top speed. He'd started to reduce contact with those particular friends. Maybe they weren't on track to be a positive influence on his life. That's why he'd been so thrilled when he'd found out about the new group for teenagers who weren't orthodox. He was unorthodox. Okay, so school tried hard to integrate him into normal lessons. But he knew he kept getting in the way, stuck in his wheelchair, particularly in science and technology lessons. And when the others went for PE, he had a physiotherapy session. That was the other reason why he'd lost contact with his light-fingered friends. On Saturday mornings he'd started a series of sessions at the local swimming pool, overseen by a specialist physio, and they were just too good to miss. Being in water, with the buoyancy it provided, was just totally amazing for someone with his spinal problems. It was like he was in a different world, one where he could be free of contraptions and machinery. One that was almost pain free. It was blissful.

He sometimes wondered if it was the medication he was on that made him feel different to everyone else, rather than just the fact he was in a wheelchair. He sometimes felt as if his brain wanted to burst out of his head, in the same way that his body wanted to burst out of his wheelchair. He was so constrained, trapped in many ways, but he couldn't afford to let it get to him. His dad kept telling him: stay calm and cheerful. Even if you don't feel it, try to be bright and positive. Then other people will react in the right way and want to be around you.

He loved his dad. And his step-mum. His real mum had walked out on them when he was still a baby, though his dad had married again. His step-mum was great, so much so that he just called her Mum to keep it simple. And she obviously liked it. He'd never really known his birth mum anyway, so what difference did it make?

Wolfie got down to work and finished his assignment before their evening meal was ready. His mum took him to the community centre this time, dropping him off at the entrance with instructions on how to contact her for his collection later. She fussed too much, though it was for all the right reasons.

'Are you sure you'll be okay, Wolfie?' she asked, one final time. She had that concerned look on her face.

'Yeah, totally,' he replied. 'All understood. Over and out. Roger. You're clear to return to base.'

He gave her a grin, so she smiled back and returned to the car. He knew that she only wanted to do the best for him, but it all got a bit much sometimes. He manoeuvred the chair through the doorway and sped down the corridor to the small community room. Everyone else was already there and a tall dark-haired woman was talking to Kerry. She must be the police detective. She was wearing trainers, jeans and a black leather jacket. She looked really cool. He steered his wheelchair across to the small cluster of people. Kerry introduced him.

'Rae, this is Wolfie. He's the last of our members.'

Wolfie grinned and raised his hand in greeting, fingers spread. 'It's a fair cop. You've got me bang to rights. I'll come quietly, guv. But can I have a bit of that fruit cake first?'

'Of course,' Rae replied, laughing. 'I made it at the weekend, so it ought to be eaten. No nuts in it though. I'm a bit allergic to nuts.'

Wolfie thought that she had a lovely voice, even though it was a bit on the deep side. Other than that, and the fact she was tall, there was no sign she was trans. He thought she was about five foot ten. But his mum was that height, so he was used to tall women.

'So am I,' he replied. 'They could ruin my life if I let them. So I just try to ignore them and hope they'll pass me by.'

She laughed again. 'I'm surprised you get bothered, with a ferocious name like Wolfie. Wolfie by name, wolfie by nature?'

He grimaced. 'Only in my dreams. I mean, if someone decides to have a go at me, what can I do about it?'

She came closer and shook his hand. 'I'm Rae, and I'm glad to meet you, Wolfie. I'm trying to learn how to bake and this is one of my experiments. You'll have to tell me what you think.'

'Mmm,' he replied, his mouth full of date loaf. 'Brill. Better than my mum's. She puts walnuts in it, though. It's that nut problem again. All her other cakes are good, though. She gets me to test them before she heads off to one of her cake sales.'

'We're in agreement about the nuts, then,' she replied. 'Thanks for the review, Mr Cake Expert.' She widened her eyes solemnly, keeping a straight face for a few seconds.

Wolfie noticed that Rowan was hanging on every word Rae uttered, eyes shining and looking awestruck. Of course. Rae was probably the first trans adult she'd ever got close to. And what a role model. It was like the time he'd been to the local athletics track for a session of wheelchair athletics and he'd met David Weir. He hadn't come down from cloud nine for days. Role models were so important in modern life, showing people like him and Rowan what could be done if you just put your mind to it.

'Let's sit down,' Kerry said. 'Rae, do you want to start?'

'I'd better say a bit about myself, hadn't I? I'm Rae Gregson, I'm a trans woman and I'm twenty-eight. I'm a detective sergeant in Dorset police's top team, the violent crime unit. It's a really responsible job because we're involved in solving crimes all across the county. Sometimes even further. On a recent big case I was in Somerset a lot, then up to Durham, Berwick and York. Some cases I can't even talk about. I love my job though. It's just the best. I met Kerry and Danny about a year ago. I'm not allowed to talk about it because the court case is coming up soon and we can't put it at risk. But they've both met my boyfriend, Craig, when we all went to Danny's music concert.'

Wolfie looked across at Danny, who was usually the quietest member of the group and whose facial expression rarely showed what he was thinking. Not just now though. He was smiling broadly and looking excited. This Rae person must really mean something to him.

'Yeah. That concert was awesome,' Kerry added. 'It was so cool to watch Danny and the others.'

Wolfie saw the way Rae looked Kerry in the eye and smiled. There was something special in their friendship,

Wolfie could see. But it would be rude to ask about it. Maybe that role model thing again.

Rae went on. 'I've brought a good torch and a couple of other bits of kit with me, so let's go and take a look.'

Chapter 7: The Abandoned Doorway

The area around the abandoned doorway was silent, with no one about. A solitary dog wandered towards them as they approached but stopped some yards short. It sniffed the air, urinated against a nearby tree and slunk away into the shadows on the other side of the road.

Rowan pointed to the grubby shop entrance. 'This is it.'

Rae took a kind of scanner out of her bag, knelt down and used it to beam a purplish glow onto the ground and some of the surfaces.

'Ultra-violet,' she explained. 'It's not the latest kit. I wouldn't be allowed to take one of those out unofficially like this. This is an old one that we use in things like school visits and lectures. It's a bit basic but it does the job.' Several spots glowed brightly on the concrete floor. 'Something here, but only slight traces. It is blood though.'

'Some of them were there when we saw her Monday night,' Rowan replied. 'Remember I said that she'd been punched or hit? Her nose was bleeding, and a couple of drops fell right there. Isn't there anything else?'

'Doesn't look like it.' Rae widened the area she'd scanned and picked up a few more stains on the pavement and the wall. 'Do you think they could have been caused at the same time?'

Kerry was unsure. 'The trouble is, it was dark. We couldn't see stuff clearly.'

Reluctantly, the group of teenagers nodded their agreement.

'But she could have been kidnapped, couldn't she?' Danny suggested. 'All that thing does is spot any blood. Someone could have grabbed her and pushed her into a van.'

Rae slid the scanner into her bag and carefully zipped it shut. 'But why, Danny? Those kinds of abductions only happen if there's a reason. A ransom or something like that. But you've all said that Daisy didn't own anything much and you don't think she had any family.'

Lee spoke up. 'But there was something going on back on Monday night, Rae. It wasn't just a couple of bullies having a go. I've been bullied like that. There was some point to it, but I don't know what it was.' He turned to Rowan. 'Don't you think so too?'

Rowan shrugged. 'I guess so. I'm not totally sure though. What about you, Josh? You were the only one who saw them twice. Do you think there was some kind of purpose behind it?'

'I think so. I've been thinking about it since. What they did,' Josh said. 'It did look a bit planned. As if they'd been put up to it. It might have been that guy standing back in the shadows when we arrived later. You ought to have a look across the road in the play area. Me and Lee both thought someone was across there, watching us on Monday night.'

The group followed Rae across the road but hung back as she entered the play park with Rowan and Kerry. She turned on the flashlight she'd been carrying and scanned the area.

'We spotted all those bags lying around,' Rowan said. 'What are they?'

Rae spotted Kerry turning her head away. The Misfit leader already knew, not surprising considering her troubled background. 'There could be a lot of reasons, but they could be from small packets of drugs. Maybe they were being sold here?'

'Does that mean Daisy was getting in the way? Once she dossed down in that doorway?' Lee asked.

'Could be,' Rae replied. 'These dealers don't like their business being upset. They can get quite vicious. I'll need to do some checking back at base tomorrow. Maybe there's a local drugs unit that have an idea what's been going on. Look, I want you all to stay away from here in case it's linked to drugs in some way. Those guys get really nasty if they think they're under threat. There's nothing else I can do at the moment.'

They headed back to the community centre.

'So what you're thinking, Rae, is that Daisy is probably alright?' Rowan was the first to speak once they were gathered together in the small meeting room.

'That's about it,' Rae said.

Kerry joined in. 'Daisy probably wasn't attacked again but it was a bit more than just a couple of knobheads having a go at her for no reason? Is that what you think?'

'Yes, that's what my guess is. She's shifted away to avoid trouble. Maybe that's what that episode was all about, to put the frighteners on her and get her to move. Did you hear anything being said on Monday, Josh?'

Josh shook his head. 'Nah. I didn't get close enough. They were muttering something to her though. So where would she have gone?'

'There are a couple of hostels for homeless people,' Kerry said. 'Maybe we should check them. Half term starts tomorrow. Maybe we should meet up if we've got nothing else arranged and check them out.'

The others agreed with this idea. The detective looked a bit uneasy.

'That sounds fine, Kerry, but I don't want any of you putting yourself in danger. Do you all understand? No going back to that doorway or hanging around that park opposite. And if you do find Daisy at one of the shelters, let me know.' She looked at the clock on the wall. 'Listen, I have to go. Kerry's asked me to come to one of your proper planned meetups. I can chat to you about your rights and what to do if you get picked on and bullied. That'll be in a month or so and I'll try to bring someone with me. Between now and then, just be sensible. Please.'

Kerry waited until Rae had left, then spoke to the others. 'She's pretty cool, isn't she?'

'I think we all liked her,' Fatima replied. 'But are we going to do exactly what she said?'

Kerry laughed. 'Listen. I'm Kerry Fenners, famous troublemaker. I do what I like, not what someone tells me. You've all gotta make your own minds up about this. We'll check out the hostels tomorrow but if we don't find her, I'm not gonna give up. I still think she was trying to write a message on that bit of paper we found. And I still think I've seen that girl who kicked her. Seen her somewhere else, but a long time ago. See, we've all been bullied like that sometime in the past. Or even now. No one should have to put up with it. See these dickheads who do it? I'm gonna find them and if they still keep doing it, I'm gonna make them sorry. So who's in?'

She looked round at the raised hands and determined faces.

'It's the first case for the Misfits,' she said. 'Let's do it!'

Chapter 8: Teamwork

The group met the next morning, the first day of the half-term holiday, in a town centre cafe that served a huge range of milkshakes, and it was here that Fatima showed her planning skills. She'd stayed very much in the background until this point, letting Kerry and Rowan, as the two organisers, take the lead.

'Any ideas how we do this?' Rowan asked, wiping banana milkshake froth from her top lip. 'Kerry and I talked about it on the way over here. We know what we want to do. Find Daisy and check that she's okay. But we're not sure how to get started.'

It was at this point that Fatima spoke up. 'I was thinking about it, last night. I think we need to split up into two or three groups, with a different task for each. If we go around as a group of seven, we'll be spotted a mile off. Two or three of us together won't be so obvious. Then there's a list of things we need to investigate, and we'll get it done quicker if we share it out.'

Kerry nodded, impressed. 'Sounds good. What things have you thought of?'

'Well, there are three obvious ones, so that's where we should start. One group checks the two hostels that Rae talked about. But we know that some homeless people don't use them. There's sometimes a group of dossers around the car park by the market, though they're never in the same place for long. There might be a few other places they use. Maybe we could ask them if they've seen her. Then another group could start doing research on the area she disappeared from and see if it's got a history of being used for dealing. I don't mean by visiting it 'cos Rae said we weren't to do that, but we could use the library to look through local newspapers. You know, use the local crime page.'

'That's a brill plan, Fatima,' Rowan said. 'You could be our planner-in-chief. So who should be in which group?'

Kerry spoke up. 'Rowan and I should check on the dossers around the market car park. We're the eldest and can look after ourselves better. It could be the biggest trouble. Maybe Fatima and Lee could do the hostels? The rest do the research? What do you think?'

'No,' Wolfie said. 'Don't leave me inside, please. I get so fed up stuck inside buildings. Can I go with one of the other groups? I love to be outside. Please. I'll probably sulk if you don't agree.'

He looked so mournful that the others started laughing.

'Okay,' Kerry said. 'We can take you with us. So that leaves Danny and Josh to do the research. Is that okay? We can swap round next time, so we all get a fair share. Did you think of other ideas, Fatima?'

'Yeah. Maybe Daisy needed to see a nurse or doctor. We ought to check out the clinic and the doctors' surgery. I can't do that 'cos my mum would blow a fuse. Maybe Josh and Danny could make a start if they get nowhere in the library. Does anyone know Daisy's surname?'

They all shook their heads.

'So we need to try and find that out. I've just thought. A couple of homeless people sometimes use the library. Maybe they could check with them while they're there.'

Josh looked much happier with this extra task.

'Anything else?' Rowan asked.

'We need to make notes, but not in an obvious way,' Fatima added. 'Not while you're talking to someone, but straight afterwards. Jot stuff down even if it doesn't sound very important. Then, when we meet up, we go through everyone's notes looking for clues.'

'Good thinking, Fatima,' Rowan said. 'So shall we meet back here at lunchtime?'

Yeah,' Wolfie said. 'the food's on me. They give a disabled discount in here and Dad gave me twenty quid when he heard I was meeting up with a group of friends. I told him you were all normal. If only he knew!'

* * *

Fatima and Lee made their way out of the cafe.

'Maybe we should have volunteered to do the research in the library,' Lee said as they crossed the road. 'Josh didn't look very happy until they got the extra bit of chatting to people in there.'

Fatima thought for a while. 'No, I think Kerry decided right. She and Rowan are talking to the dossers near the market and they're the eldest. We're next and we're doing the hostels. Danny doesn't find it easy to chat to people and Josh is pretty quiet. You don't want them in an awkward situation with people who might be drunk or high on something. Danny will be good in the library. He said he was good at internet research so it should be just right for him. And Josh can be a bit nervous, even though he told us he isn't. What do you think of Kerry and Rowan?'

'I think they're great,' Lee replied. 'They kind of rescued me from three bullies last week on my way home from school. Kerry is so tough. She's not afraid of anyone or anything. She thumped Blagger Banks really hard and he went off crying. It was amazing. Do you know him?'

'Yeah, unfortunately. He's the worst bully in our year. He picked on me sometimes, but he backed off a bit when I told one of my teachers. Did she really hit him? I wish I could have been there to see it.'

Lee smiled at the memory. 'She got him twice. Have you seen that Nicola Adams when she boxes at the Olympics? I reckon Kerry's been watching her on YouTube. It was just like that. A punch in the chest then one in the face but it was so quick. It was like a flash. I wonder if she goes to boxing lessons or something. She used to get into real trouble, Kerry did. She used to get drunk and get into fights down in the town at night. And she was meant to do all kinds of stuff with boys. Dunno whether it was true or not and I'm too scared to ask.'

Fatima laughed. 'You're such an innocent, Lee. I've done stuff, but not with boys. I told you I liked other girls. My mum would go mad if she knew that so you gotta forget that I told you, okay? But Kerry is kind of mixed up still, that's what I think. You don't really get over it when your dad is killed like mine, and both her parents got killed in that house fire. I know she's said she didn't like them, but even so. I really like Rowan.

She is so totally cool. She always seems calm and she thinks a lot.'

Lee looked at her. 'I bet you're the cleverest one in the group though. You're the brainbox. It was you that came up with the plan this morning.'

Fatima shrugged. 'Well, we'll see.' She looked up at the building in front of them. 'We're here. Let's get started.'

The hostel was run by a local charity that got some of its funds from a shop in the town centre that sold second-hand clothes and other goods. There was a notice beside the front door asking for donations and listing the kind of items that sold well.

'It says that DVDs make really good donations,' Lee said. 'I've never been in their shop. Maybe I should look to see what they've got.'

'What, films or music ones?' Fatima asked.

Lee shrugged. 'Films, really. But I like music ones too.'

They looked up as the door opened and a man emerged onto the top step. 'Yes? Can I help you?'

Fatima explained. 'We're looking for our friend Daisy. She's a rough sleeper but she's gone missing from the doorway she used, round the back of the community centre. We take her soup and biscuits, and we're a bit worried about her. We wondered if she was here.'

The man on the step looked wary. 'How old is she?'

'We don't know exactly but we think she's about thirty or forty. She's got fair hair.'

The man shook his head. 'No. We don't have anyone called Daisy and no-one with that description. You could try the other hostel, down on the south side of the town centre.'

'Okay, thanks,' Fatima replied.

Lee just smiled. They turned away and walked back down the street.

'Maybe this will be shorter than we thought,' Lee said. 'If the next one isn't any better, we could go to the library and help the others.'

The next hostel wasn't any better. In fact, the warden had a hostile manner and refused to answer any questions or give them any information at all. Lee felt downhearted but Fatima was more upbeat.

'I hoped we'd get some information about Daisy,' she said. 'But I kind of guessed that this might happen. Some of the people in these hostels are scared, especially the women. Some have been beaten up for years by their partners and they've only just escaped. And the wardens know that some really vicious men get up to all kinds of tricks to find out where they are. They've got to protect the inmates, so they don't let any information out.'

'So she could be in there? Is that what you mean?'

'Yeah. It's possible. Anyway, let's get back to see how Josh and Danny have got on.'

Chapter 9: In the Library

Josh had been disappointed with the task he and Danny had been allocated. He wanted to be outside doing some real detective work, not stuck inside a dull library, reading stuff. Had he been picked for this job because he was black? That was so unfair. He complained to Danny but didn't really get anywhere. Danny just shrugged and said that Kerry knew what she was doing and, anyway, the suggestion had come from Fatima. She wouldn't be a racist, would she?

Josh moped silently as they made their way to the library. Danny obviously knew the librarian and she gave him some ideas to get started and told him which computer to use. He got stuck in so quickly that Josh couldn't help but be impressed, but Josh himself still felt a bit left out. It was then that he saw a couple of really untidy people over in one corner, sitting reading magazines. Were these the dosser-people Fatima had mentioned? He decided to investigate.

The two both had plastic carrier bags beside them, stuffed full of what looked to be bedding quilts and spare clothes. They didn't smell too bad, just a damp, mildewy whiff. Josh spoke up.

'Excuse me. Do you know someone called Daisy? She sometimes slept in a shop doorway round the back of the community centre. I'm looking for her.'

The man looked at Josh warily. 'Why?' He had a gruff voice.

'Cos my friends and me are a bit worried about her. She's gone missing.'

The man shrugged. 'Mebbe she's just wandered off 'cos she felt like it. What's it to you?'

'She got punched a few days ago.'

The man laughed. 'Nowt new there. We get picked on all the time, don't we, Bets?'

The woman coughed. 'Did she have a big spot on her chin?' Her voice was rough, as if she had a sore throat.

'Yeah, that's her.'

Bets coughed again, then sneezed into her sleeve. 'Yeah, I've seen her around but not this week. Like Charlie said, folks come and go all the time. You gotta get used to it. Most of us just wanna be left alone. We're better off that way.'

'Do you know anything else about her?'

Josh felt their eyes on him as if they were trying to probe his mind, looking for some bad intention on his part. They shook their heads then looked back down at their magazines as if to say, *this conversation is over*.

Josh returned to the desk where Danny was still working and wrote a description of the couple and a record of what they'd said in his notebook. He knew the woman's name was Bets, but he'd forgotten to ask the man's name. He turned back to the corner where they'd been sitting, meaning to walk back across and ask them. They'd gone. Their chairs were empty, and a library assistant was putting the magazines they'd been reading back into a rack. He was puzzled. They must have left because of his questions, but why? Did that mean that they knew more about Daisy than they'd let on? He told Danny what had happened, but Danny just looked puzzled.

'I'm rubbish at guessing why people do things,' he said. 'It's cos of my Asperger's. Look, I've found a lot.'

Josh looked down at Danny's pad and saw a list of dates and people's names, with a short note beside each.

'There's drugs stuff been going on for ages and that area's been really bad. Police clear it but they come back again. People have been beaten up there before.'

'Wow. You found all that out from the local paper? That's really good.'

'It's all important, Josh. See, this kind of stuff helps detectives. That's what Rae tells us. I bet we've found out as much in here as the others do.'

Josh looked up as the main door opened. Fatima and Lee walked in, looking a bit dejected. Maybe Danny was right.

'No luck,' Fatima said as they sat down. 'We didn't really get anywhere.'

'Fatima thinks they wouldn't tell us, even if Daisy was in a hostel,' Lee said. 'It might put her in danger if word got out, so they keep quiet. Makes sense, I s'pose.'

They added their notes to the two sheets that already lay on the desktop. Then all four of them spent time reading what had been listed.

'It's not much, is it?' Josh said. He looked disappointed.

Fatima answered him sharply. 'Well, you got more than we did. But did you really think we'd get to the bottom of it right away, Josh? It doesn't work like that. It'll take days, and even then, we might not find out where she is. Anyway, we've still got to find out how the other three got on. I think they might have a better chance than Lee and me.'

They gathered their stuff together and headed outside. It was time to head back to the café to see how Kerry, Rowan and Wolfie had got on. They imagined that, somehow, those three might have shaken things up a bit when they interviewed people. After all, they were the three most lively members of the group and, in Kerry, they had someone who seemed afraid of nothing.

Chapter 10: Friction at the Market

Wolfie's wheelchair came whizzing down the slope towards the market with all three of the teenagers on it. Wolfie himself, of course, was sitting in the seat, as expected. Kerry was perched in front, trying to balance herself on the footstep, almost sitting on Wolfie's lap. Rowan was at the back, supposedly pushing, but she had raised her feet onto part of the frame and was holding on tightly. In fact, there was little danger. The slope wasn't very steep and levelled out at the end as the footpath approached the market area.

'Wow. That was fun,' Kerry said. 'Did you see the face of that woman with the shopping? She glared daggers at us as we passed. Maybe you need to fit a bell, Wolfie.'

'It might need a service soon,' he replied. 'It was creaking a bit back there. I'd better tell Dad and maybe he can get a warning bell put on somewhere. I'd better not mention this little trip though. Maybe it was under strain with all three of us on it.'

'Yeah, but we'll have to push you back up the hill, won't we?' Rowan added. 'S'only fair for you to give us a lift here.'

They made their way towards the covered car park behind the market, heading for the corner at the rear of the baker's shop. Its ovens kept the back wall warm, attracting a number of the town's rough sleepers. Warmth was something so many people took for granted but sleeping outside during the colder months gave homeless folk a different perspective on its importance. Kerry waved at one of the figures as the trio approached the cluster of people sitting on a low wall, surrounded by grimy quilts and sleeping bags. The air smelled musty and stale.

'Well, look who's here. It's young Kerry Fenners. Mad, bad and dangerous.' The speaker, a husky voiced woman who looked about fifty, gave a throaty laugh. 'Haven't seen you for some time, gal. You alright?'

'Yeah. I got a pie for you to share, Togs.' Kerry passed a paper bag across to the woman.

'Where you bin all this time? You shifted somewhere since your ma and pa died?'

Kerry nodded. 'We're with Gramps now. I don't booze anymore, Togs. Not so much, anyway. I decided to go to college and try to get some qualifications. I don't do the mad, bad and dangerous thing now. It was all a bit pathetic, really.'

Togs nodded, as if she were an expert on such things. 'Very wise. Very *sagacious*. Who are your friends?'

'Well, this is Wolfie in the wheelchair. And this is my best friend, Rowan. Guys, this is Togs, named after her love of high-class clothing.'

The other two youngsters looked at the grubby rags that Togs was wearing. Had her clothes been designer wear at some time in the distant past? It was impossible to say. Those coloured bits on her coat could be the remains of a pattern but could equally well be stains of some type.

Kerry continued. 'Then the others are Ken, Gobbie and Toast. I won't explain why they're called that. It would take too long.' She switched her attention back to Togs. 'We're trying to find someone, Togs. She's a homeless person like you. Her name's Daisy and she disappeared a few days ago. She used to sleep in a shop doorway near the back of the Community Centre. We're a bit worried about her. Can you help?'

Togs looked at her three companions. There was a shake of the head from Ken and Toast, but Gobbie scowled.

'Okay, Gobbie. Go ahead. Kerry is a pal, so we can trust her.'

Kerry didn't let on that she already knew Gobbie, nor that she was wary of him.

Gobbie coughed and spat. He was tall and gangly, and his voice was throaty and weak, as if his lungs were filled with catarrh. 'Knew her a bit.' Cough. 'Didn't wanna mix with us.' Cough. 'Alright though.' Spit. 'A loner.'

'Do you know why she might have moved away?' Rowan asked.

He shook his head. 'Wouldn't have gone far. Local girl.' Cough.

Rowan went on. 'That doorway she was living in. There's a small park opposite. Could she have got into trouble just by being there?'

Togs bit her lip. 'Could be. It's not a good place for the likes of us. It looks okay, but some nasties hang around there. We stay away.'

'Would Daisy have known that? If she's local she should have, shouldn't she? I mean, you know about it.'

Togs shrugged. 'Dunno. Maybe she had a reason.'

61

Ken spoke up. 'I heard she got chucked out of where she was staying for being pissed all the time. Mebbe she had no choice.'

Wolfie joined in. 'Why didn't she come down here with you lot? She'd have been warmer.'

Gobbie stared at him. 'Cos she stole twenty quid from me last time I saw her. Spent it on booze and drank it all herself. Bloody thief.' He coughed and spat.

The others looked at him. 'Didn't know that,' Togs said.

'Kept it to meself, didn't I?' Gobbie coughed. 'Gotta have some secrets.' He turned and walked away.

The other three looked at each other. Toast, a short man whose hair stuck up in the air like a lavatory brush, spoke. He had a posh-sounding voice. 'Well, what's got into him? I think you've touched a nerve, young man.' He looked at Togs. 'Are you going to share that pie out, dearest? I think it's about time for luncheon. Shall I get the serviettes out?' He winked at the teenagers.

Togs waited until Gobbie was out of earshot, then turned to Kerry. 'Listen. I'll find out what I can, okay? That's the best I can do. Come back in a couple of days.'

The trio of teenagers set out on the long uphill haul back to the café, with the two girls taking it in turns to push Wolfie's wheelchair.

'Hope the others have found out more than us,' Kerry said. 'That was a bit disappointing.'

Rowan disagreed. 'We got more than you think. That Gobbie knew something. He walked off cos he didn't want to answer any more questions. We need to keep an eye on him.'

'That might be hard,' Kerry said. 'He's seen us all now. He'll get suspicious if he sees us hanging around. I dunno why he was there. He's not homeless. At least, I don't think he is.' She looked troubled.

'He won't know the others,' Wolfie said. 'It's only us three he'll know. Maybe Josh could take over. He fancies himself as a spy.'

'When did he say that?' Rowan asked.

'It was last night after Rae had left. He told me he fancied being an undercover cop and spying on crooks.'

'Gobbie is a real racist, Wolfie,' Kerry said. 'He can be really nasty. We can't put Josh in danger. Or Fatima. Lee could do it.'

'Josh is gonna be so gutted. We can't keep giving him the boring stuff to do. Maybe Fatima will come up with another plan.'

Chapter 11: Toasties

Toasted sandwiches are yummy, Rowan thought as she bit into her ham, cheese and chopped onion snack. Warm, melted cheese started to dribble down her chin so she tried to poke her tongue out far enough to lick it back. Some escaped so she wiped her skin with a finger. She looked around hoping that the others hadn't noticed and saw that some of them had similar problems. Wolfie had a ketchup smear on his top lip and Danny was trying to slurp some chopped tomato back into his mouth.

Rowan licked her lips after she finished her last mouthful. 'That was brill,' she said. 'Thanks, Wolfie.'

The others mouthed their appreciation and Kerry burped.

'S'okay,' Wolfie said. 'This is so great for someone like me, to get out like this. Maybe we can do pizzas next time?'

Rowan grinned. 'Sure. Now can we get a bit of feedback from everyone? Do you wanna start, Fatima?'

'Here are our notes,' Fatima replied, pushing a slip of paper into the middle of the table. 'Not much to report, though. We think the warden at the first hostel was telling us the truth. He was helpful and told us he'd keep an eye open for Daisy. The second one was a bit different. The warden there hardly said anything. She was being really careful. But it has some places reserved for women who've escaped from men who've been beating them up, so we could see why she didn't want to tell us much.'

Lee broke in. 'But we still wondered if she knew something. We could try again if we get stuck everywhere else. That's what we thought.'

'Good thinking, 'Rowan said. 'And well done. See, getting no information is still good. It tells us where she probably isn't, so we just tick that place off. How about you two?' She turned to Josh and Danny.

Josh swallowed his last mouthful of milkshake. 'Danny did brill. He found a lot about that playpark opposite the doorway. There's a list of stuff from the paper of trouble around there, so we think we were right. It's been used by pushers for a while. The cops clear people away but they just come back. Here's Danny's list. I had a chat with some trampy people in the library and one of them knew Daisy. But she doesn't know where she is now. I kind-of believe her. Why would she lie? Her name's Bets. We haven't been into the clinic yet.'

Kerry was next. 'Rowan, me and Wolfie got on okay at the market carpark. I knew the four scruffies there. Two of them were okay and tried to help us. That was Togs and Toast. Ken didn't say anything so I dunno about him. He never says much. Rowan thinks that the last one, Gobbie, knows something. He walked off in a huff. I dunno what to do about him cos he can be nasty if he wants to be. But if he does know something about Daisy, we'll need to watch him. You know, keep him under surveillance or whatever the word is.'

Rowan spoke up. 'Yeah. I think he was a bit odd, but he did say that Daisy had pinched twenty quid from him. He got angry about it. That's why he walked off in

65

a mood. I didn't like him. He looks like he could be a bit of a bully.'

Wolfie frowned. 'Yeah, but what if Daisy really did pinch twenty quid from him? You can understand him getting angry about it. We all would, wouldn't we?'

'I dunno, Wolfie,' Rowan replied. 'I mean you're right. But Daisy never came across as the type who'd be a thief. Would she steal money from someone?'

'We don't know,' Fatima said. 'None of us knew her well enough.'

Danny spoke for the first time. 'But if she's a thief, do we want to help her? Why are we bothering?'

Rowan was taken aback. 'We don't know that, Danny. He could've been lying to throw us off the scent. I know we only talked to Daisy for a short while, but I liked her. And until we know for definite, we ought to keep looking for her. If she did steal dosh from him it was probably to get food or something. These people are starving most of the time. But I reckon he was lying. He looked shifty.'

Kerry was frowning. 'Danny, Gobbie was one of Dad's pals. He can be really nasty. We gotta be careful with him.' She glanced around. 'So what do we do now? Any ideas?'

They looked at each other's glum faces. The upbeat enthusiasm of the morning had gone, and they were all feeling dispirited at the lack of progress. Even Wolfie had nothing to say and looked tired. Fatima guessed what the problem was.

'We should have expected this,' she said. 'We all hoped we'd find her this morning or get a clue about where she is. But that was a bit stupid. Detectives never expect to find a missing person this quick, on the first day. That's what Rae said. We've just got to keep at it and not give up. All we've got to do is come up with another plan. We need other places to check out this afternoon. What about going to the train station to see if anyone remembers her going away?'

They started to perk up.

Josh spoke. 'Yeah, and the bus station. That might be better 'cos bus travel's cheaper and she won't have much dosh.'

'My local church does a sort of soup-kitchen for dossers,' Wolfie said. 'My mum helps sometimes. Is that worth checking?'

Kerry was smiling again. 'Yeah. It's all good. But we mustn't get our hopes up too high this time. It was kinda fun this morning but we gotta take it seriously. And I reckon Rowan's right. That Gobbie is a real liar. He's a bit of a snake but we need to watch him in case he knows something. Who can do that best?'

Danny chipped in. 'I know who he is so I can do it. I remember he came to the house once to see our Dad. It was ages ago.' He was silent for a few moments. 'I'll need someone with me, though.'

Fatima was the first to volunteer. 'I'll do it, even if he is a racist moron. I've met enough of those in the two years I've been here. Okay, Danny? It means you and me can get to know each other. So it looks as though we split into three again. That's good. It worked this morning, didn't it?'

They'd got their enthusiasm back and it showed. Some final arrangements were made about staying in contact, then they left, one group at a time. The search for news of Daisy was back on!

* * *

The café door closed behind the last of the teenagers and the woman who'd been sipping a cup of tea while sitting at a small side table, set down her magazine. She'd used it to help hide herself while trying to overhear what they were talking about, but she'd failed to follow what they said. The only clear words that had reached her were the names Daisy and Gobbie. She was annoyed. Teenagers were usually too loud when they talked but this lot had kept their voices down. They were up to something. She knew it. They were meddling and might find out too much. That would cause a problem. She didn't quite know what to do, though. She slipped on her black coat, picked up her bag and hurried to the door. She'd think of a way to stay one step ahead of them, though it might take a while for a good idea to occur to her.

She stepped outside into the cool October air. There were some of them, in the distance, just separating into two groups. Who should she follow? She opted for the boy in the wheelchair. He'd be easy to shadow. After all, who could possibly lose track of something as big and ponderous as a wheelchair? That trio of teenagers wouldn't be able to dodge down narrow alleys or nip across busy roads. They couldn't suddenly rush up an escalator in a department store, then double-back down the stairs. It would be easy for her. She put her hood up to hide her features and ambled slowly along the road towards the top of the hill, deliberately hanging back. She reached the brow and looked down the slope. The wheelchair was nowhere to be seen.

Where had it gone? Maybe into a house? She hurried down the slope, peering into each driveway as she passed by, but spotted nothing. She'd lost them and couldn't understand why. She swore and, in a fit of bad temper, kicked at a stone lying on the pavement at a driveway entrance.

It wasn't a stone. It was a small upright metal plate, partly sunk into the surface to catch the down bolts on the driveway gates when they were closed. She shrieked in pain and limped to the garden wall to take a rest. Her foot hurt abominably, and several people stopped to ask her if she was alright. Infuriatingly, she realised that two of them were the two tall girls from the group of teenagers. How had they got behind her? They must have called into a shop immediately after leaving the café. She knew her face had gone red and that tears were wetting her cheeks. Had they heard her swearing?

She waved off all offers of help and limped away towards her small flat. Had she broken her toe? It certainly felt like it and it needed to be checked. She just hoped that she wouldn't need to visit the local hospital for an x-ray. Things were far too busy, and she had no time to spare. By the time she approached her home, the pain was almost unbearable. She gritted her teeth and tried to hold back the tears. This was all going wrong because of those pesky teenagers.

Chapter 12: Racial Abuse

Fatima was already thinking things through, even as she and Danny separated from the others a few hundred metres from the café. Kerry and Rowan had gone into a small bookshop to buy a street map of the town. Josh, Lee and Wolfie headed off east towards the bus station.

'Kerry said that this Gobbie person walked away in the opposite direction to the shops. Where would that take him, Danny? Remember they were in the car park at the back of the market. You must know the town better than me. You've lived here all your life.'

Danny was good at logical thinking, probably better than his sister. He guessed it was somehow linked to his Asperger's. The thing he had trouble with was trying to understand people's moods and how, when they spoke, they often meant the exact opposite of what they actually said. It was like learning another language but one that was hidden. Like when people said, *Hello. It's good to see you. You look well.* And they didn't mean that at all. He'd never worked out quite what they did mean by it. He'd come to the conclusion that they didn't mean anything. Half of the stuff that adults said to him was just meaningless, just empty words. Just being polite. At least these new pals said what they meant.

'The train station's in that direction. And the community centre.'

'So that means the doorway that Daisy was in is up that way?'

'Yeah. And that manky playpark with the bushes and stuff. But sometimes dossers meet up near the footbridge over the railway. Gramps told me not to go along that way alone because of it.'

Fatima was silent for a few moments. Danny guessed she was thinking hard. He'd been really impressed with Fatima since the group had met on Monday night. Awestruck even. He'd never met anyone of his age who thought things through so carefully as her. The teenager he knew best was his sister, Kerry. And she'd been totally wild until the last year. She'd spent her early teenage years in moody confrontations, reacting to the mayhem of their life at home with a drunken mother and a thuggish father. And when she'd begun drinking herself, things had got really bad. He daren't tell his new friends the kind of stuff that Kerry had got up to in the past. She'd become the unofficial leader of the Misfits and he could see how she loved being in that role. If they found out what she used to be like, would they even want her still in the group?

He realised that Fatima had begun talking.

'We could go to the station first and see if he's there. Last time I went to London with Mum we saw some scruffy men in a side road. They were drinking cans of strong beer. Mum thought it was awful. They called us migrant spongers and told us to get back to where we came from. She got really angry.'

'What happened?'

'She told them she was a doctor at the local clinic and that she'd already treated one of them for cuts and bruises after a fight. She said she wouldn't use an

71

anaesthetic on him next time but just sew him up without painkillers. He shut up then.' Fatima laughed and Danny couldn't help laughing too.

'Do you go to London much?'

'Not really. We don't have enough money. But we go once a year to visit the museums. Mum thinks it's really important that we learn as much as we can about all kinds of stuff. She says that knowledge is power. I think she's right. Those idiots who swore at us were that way because they hadn't bothered learning stuff at school. They're ignorant. They don't understand other people and cultures and they're frightened of things they don't understand.'

Danny was listening carefully to what Fatima was saying. It made sense. 'So is that why I get picked on sometimes? Cos people don't understand my Asperger's?'

Fatima nodded. 'I expect so. Does it happen much?'

He shook his head. 'Nah. They all know Kerry's my sister. She's not scared of anything. If anyone picks on me, she just jumps them, and they end up in a mess. It hasn't happened for ages though. They all learnt.'

Fatima laughed. 'She does have a reputation. I even heard of her, and I go to a different school to you. Mad Kerry Fenners. That's what she was called.'

By this time, they were approaching the station. A couple scruffy looking men with dogs were sprawled against a wall around the corner from the station concourse but Gobbie wasn't with them. The two teenagers walked past, heading for the footbridge further along the road.

'Hey, darlin,' one of the men called. 'You need a good wash. Your skin's dirty and brown. I can get you some bleach if you wannit.'

Fatima stopped walking, turned and spoke calmly to him. 'I'm telling the police what you've just said.' She pulled out her phone and dialled 999.

* * *

Rowan and Kerry arrived at the bus station ten minutes after leaving the café. They had a good look round to see if Daisy was there, hidden away in one of the darker corners, but there seemed to be no homeless people or beggars around. Maybe the staff at the bus station were super-efficient at moving people on. They wouldn't want visitors to the town, newly arrived after a bus trip, to be greeted by rows of people slumped on dirty pavements, begging.

The two girls made their way to the bus station office and described who they were looking for. The supervisor was a middle-aged man with greying hair, but he looked to be a thoughtful type of person.

'Her name's Daisy,' Rowan said. 'Has anyone like her left on a long-distance bus in the last couple of days?'

'I keep my eye on things and no-one of that description has been around for a while now. I'm not here in the evenings though. If she got a late bus I wouldn't know. But good luck with your search.'

The two girls were surprised at how helpful he'd been and told him so.

He frowned. 'I was homeless once, a long time ago. I remember what it was like, kipping down on a bench. It was the worst time of my life and I wouldn't wish it on anybody.'

Kerry was distracted by the ringing of her mobile phone. She listened to the caller with a look of surprise and worry on her face.

'What?' she said. 'Are you both okay, Danny?'

She pocketed her phone and turned to Rowan.

'That was Danny. He and Fatima are in an office at the train station. The cops are there interviewing them. Some bastard had a go at Fatima. We need to check they're okay.'

The supervisor spoke. 'There's a bus leaving in a minute and it goes past the station. I'll get you on it for free.'

The two girls were at the station within five minutes, looking for someone who could help them locate Danny and Fatima. A police squad car was parked outside the main entrance, so they hurried inside and spoke to a community officer standing to one side. She was reluctant to let them into the office being used to interview the two younger teenagers until Kerry told her that Danny had Asperger's and would clam up when he got stressed.

Once they were inside, they were surprised to see both Danny and Fatima looking relaxed and cheerful. They were each sipping at cups of hot chocolate and munching on gingernut biscuits. A police constable was tidying things away, clearly about to leave. A woman was standing in one corner, talking on a mobile phone. Was she Fatima's mother?

'Is one of you his older sister?' the police officer asked.

'Me, I'm Kerry. Are you okay, Danny?'

Danny grinned. 'Yeah. See Fatima? She did everything totally right, that's what they said.'

The policeman explained. 'We'll be charging the offender with racist hate crime. He's already been taken to the police station. These two have behaved in a very mature and sensible way. Danny's a real credit, Kerry. If other people reacted like these two did, we'd find it easier to bring charges against people. But we were lucky that someone else overheard and is willing to act as an independent witness. It'll make it easy to prosecute.' He stopped talking and looked more carefully at Kerry. 'Don't I know you from somewhere?'

She sighed. 'Yeah, probably. I used to get into trouble. Maybe it was that.'

He shook his head. 'Don't think so. Were you the two who escaped that house file last winter? I was on duty that night.'

Kerry just nodded. 'We're living with our Gramps now.'

'Well, I have all the details I need.' He turned to Fatima. 'You, young lady, have been a credit to the community. I've got your details, so we'll be in contact with your mum very soon.' He gathered his stuff together and left.

The woman had finished her phone call and walked across. 'Do you want to go home now, Fatima? I have the car outside.'

'No, Mum. I'm fine. We were on our way somewhere and we still need to check it out. I'll be home later in the afternoon, like I said this morning. Don't worry, I'll be fine. These are my friends, Rowan and Kerry. Kerry is Danny's sister.'

Fatima's mother shook their hands and left. Kerry was surprised that she'd seemed so calm.

'She knows I can look after myself,' Fatima explained. 'When you've lived through a war with the army trying to kill you every day, this kind of stuff is pretty easy to deal with.'

Chapter 13: A Spy

Wolfie, Josh and Lee had headed towards one of the town's parish churches, well known for helping the homeless. Once again, Wolfie's wheelchair was used as a group transporter and all three of them whizzed down the hill to the church. Volunteers ran a soup-kitchen at lunchtimes, using produce donated by local supermarkets. Wolfie brought the other two up to date on how it worked as they made their way through the town centre's largest park, moving more slowly now they were on foot, with Josh pushing.

'Some of the stuff is just past its best-before date, but my mum says it's still good,' Wolfie said. 'And the meat comes from that butcher along the High Street. He keeps some back and asks customers to donate some. It's a really good system. I sometimes go along and help, and the soup is great. They sometimes do sandwiches as well.'

'What about the homeless people? What are they like?' Josh asked. 'I'd never met any before Daisy. Not up close, anyway.'

Wolfie wrinkled his nose. 'They can smell a bit. You know, sort of damp and stale. My Mum say's its mildew. If it's too bad they're told to choose some new clothes from a storage cupboard in the hall. And they can get a shower. The old clothes get burned. I did that job once with a volunteer bloke. It was the mankiest thing I've ever done. Gross.'

Lee spoke. 'Yeah, but they can't help it can they? If they don't have a home, they can't get clean or wash their stuff. People with a home are bound to be cleaner. Stands to reason.'

They went around the church building to the back where the door to the hall was open, with several people sitting in the porch.

'You're a bit late, Wolfie,' an elderly woman said. 'Most people have been and gone.'

'I'm not volunteering today, Mrs Davis,' Wolfie answered. 'I'm doing something else with my friends, Josh and Lee. But you might be able to help us. We're looking for a woman who's a rough sleeper, to check she's okay. Her name's Daisy, she has a big spot on her chin and might have some sticking plasters on her face. Does any of that ring a bell?'

Mrs Davis shook her head, looking serious. 'No, not recently anyway. There might have been someone like that a couple of weeks ago. You'll need to ask one of the organisers. They keep records.'

They went into the main room and saw that most of the volunteers were packing things away. Wolfie explained. 'Lunch usually starts early, at about twelve, and is over within an hour or two. There'll be a bit left for any stragglers but most of them will have been and gone. Maybe that's good if we want to chat.'

He looked around and finally spotted the person he was looking for, a tall thin woman with short grey hair.

'Hello, Wolfie,' she said as they approached. 'I don't think we were expecting you today.'

'That's okay, Mrs O'Rourke. We're here to ask you something. This is Josh and Lee, by the way. They're friends of mine.' He pointed to them each in turn.

'We're looking for someone and wondered if she might be here or if you know anything about where she might be. She's a rough sleeper called Daisy. It's just that she's gone missing and we're worried about her. We want to check that she's okay.'

Mrs O'Rourke stopped in her task of wiping down a table. 'Well, we did have someone called Daisy Shaw here a couple of times earlier in the month, but not recently. Why? Why shouldn't she be okay?'

'We think she was kicked around a bit by a couple of louts, just a few days ago. We're keeping an eye open for her. We'll tell the police if we find her so they can check she's fine.'

'Well, that's very laudable, Wolfie. But I can't help you, I'm afraid. We only ever ask for someone's name. If they want to give us an address, then that's fine but we don't insist. What would be the point? People like Daisy can't give us an address, can they?'

Josh was looking around the hall. There were still a couple of street people finishing off their soup, wiping their bowls clean with crusts of bread.

'Would it be okay if we ask them if they know Daisy?'

'Normally I'd say no, that people deserve some privacy, but I trust Wolfie and I can see you're all genuinely worried about her. Go ahead, but don't be too pushy.'

The three teenagers moved across to the solitary table left in place, with two untidy-looking people finishing their hurried lunch.

'Looks like someone else has come across to interview us again, milady. Should I put on my dickie bow, do you think?' the man said, raising his bushy eyebrows in mock surprise.

'Sorry,' Wolfie said. 'You're the ones we spoke to this morning about Daisy. I didn't realise.'

Togs frowned. 'I've never been as popular as her. I bet people wouldn't go looking for me if I went walkabout for a few days.'

The man looked shocked. 'Of course I would, dearest. I would most certainly be heartbroken if you left me without warning.'

'We asked around a bit after Kerry and you left. Didn't find out nuthin', though. Nearly made us miss our lunch.'

'A feast too good to forego,' Toast added. 'A repast fit for the gods themselves. Epicurean delights of epic proportions.'

'Shut up, Toast. You can really get on my tits, you know.'

Toast pretended to zip his lips shut with his fingers.

The three teenagers left them to finish their food in peace.

'Where to now?' Wolfie asked.

Lee shrugged, but Josh made a suggestion. 'Maybe the hospital, then the health centre? Now we know her last name, there's a bit more to go on. It won't sound so bad, will it, asking if she's been in?'

Josh sent a text message to all the others telling them Daisy's surname, then they left the church and headed east towards the community hospital. When they arrived, Lee spoke to the nurse on reception.

'We're looking for Daisy Shaw, a rough sleeper. We're worried about her. She's gone missing. Has she been in for treatment?'

'I couldn't possibly tell you that,' the receptionist replied. 'It's personal information.'

'Yeah, but she got beaten up on Monday night and we haven't been able to find her since,' Lee went on. 'We just want to check she's okay.'

'Well, that's very laudable,' came the reply. 'But surely that's a matter for the police. Do they know? I'd be allowed to give them information.'

'We're working with them, with a detective. It's just that she's busy.'

'She's hired you as her deputies, has she? The answer's still the same. I can't help you, whether you're working with the police or not. I would need to see this detective herself, with identity card. Then I might be able to help her. Now there are people behind you in the queue, so please leave.' She glared at them over her glasses.

Josh pushed the wheelchair towards the door, just as it opened and a woman in a black coat came into the waiting area. She was hobbling and using a walking stick. She stared angrily at them as they passed.

'What's got her so het up?' Josh asked.

'Who? The receptionist?' Wolfie replied.

'No. That woman. She looked daggers at us.'

Lee spoke up. 'She was at the next table to us when we were having lunch. She might have been listening to what we said.'

Josh turned around and quietly slipped back into the reception area, pretending to read a set of notices on the wall. Luckily, he was partly hidden from view by a large pot plant. The woman in the black coat was talking to the receptionist.

'Phyllis Prince. I need to see someone about my toe. It might be broken.' Her voice seemed snappy. Maybe she was in pain.

'You've got a short wait. Take a seat across there.' The receptionist pointed to a row of chairs with her pen. 'Someone will call you.'

'What did those boys want?' Phyllis Prince asked.

'Why? Were they pestering you?'

'No. I just wondered. I thought I recognised one of them.'

The receptionist just shook her head, swivelled her pen round and returned to her work. Phyllis Prince glared daggers at her before moving off slowly towards the chairs. Josh slipped back outside before he was spotted.

'Well, that was interesting,' he said to the other two. 'Her name is Phyllis Prince and she's got a broken toe. That's why she's hobbling and needs to see the doctor. And then she asked about us. But get this. The receptionist wouldn't tell her anything about us. I thought she was angry with us, but it's more like she's on our side.'

Lee broke in. 'They're not allowed to tell anyone personal or medical stuff without permission. They'd get the sack.'

82

'Yeah, that makes sense. Anyway, that woman Phyllis sounds really nasty. Why would she be asking about us?'

'I reckon she was spying on us at lunch,' Lee said. 'Honestly, she was only pretending to read the magazine she had on the table. She didn't turn the page once all the time we were there. What do you think we should do now?'

Wolfie spoke up. 'Go back and tell the others? We've got somewhere, haven't we? We got two names, Daisy's other name, Shaw, and that woman, Phyllis Prince. Maybe we can do some proper investigating now.'

Lee was thinking hard. What would Fatima suggest if she were here? 'You two go back. I'm gonna wait around here and then follow her. We need to know more about her and why she's interested in us. It'll be better if I do it on my own. You two can be spotted too easily. I've got my phone, so I'll text you to let you know where I am. That's the best plan.'

Josh was unhappy about the idea. 'We shouldn't split up, Lee. I'll call the others and see if someone can come and join you. Maybe Danny. He won't be easily spotted. The rest of us could be. I'm black, Wolfie's in his wheelchair, Rowan's tall and Kerry could never merge quietly into the background, not in a million years. Fatima might be okay, but Danny's the best bet. Let's wait over by those bushes so we won't be spotted when she comes out. Okay?'

Lee thought this was a good idea. 'Yeah, of course.'

Josh phoned Fatima, told her what had happened and listened carefully to her advice. 'Wow,' he said. 'That's such a brill idea. You're a genius, Fatima.'

He turned to the others. 'Okay, this is what we're gonna do. You'll love it!'

Chapter 14: The Follower

Phyllis Prince came out of the hospital, buttoned up her coat and took some more tentative steps towards the road. The doctor was right. The pain in her toe was receding as the painkiller that she'd been given began to take effect. Luckily the toe wasn't broken, just badly bruised. It was likely to be painful for several days, so a pack of tablets was nestling securely in Phyllis's bag, with an instruction to take one every four hours.

She was still angry. Once again, she'd come across those pesky teenagers but, as before, she'd lost them. She'd been in the examination room for well over half an hour. They'd have scattered far and wide by now. There was little chance that she'd come across any of them soon. It would be a case of keeping alert for the next few days at cafés, parks and other places where nuisance teenagers congregated. It was all such a complete pain in the neck. Why had they got involved anyway, stirring up trouble with everyone? Bloody do-gooders.

She put her gloves on, straightened her hat and walked tentatively to the main road where she stopped and looked around her. She'd only taken a few steps when she suddenly stopped, unable to believe what she was seeing. The boy in the wheelchair was about forty yards ahead of her, near an open grassy area. She moved behind a convenient tree and watched, trying to make out what was going on. The black boy with him had what looked to be a bag of crisps in his hand and was nibbling on a few. It got handed to the wheelchair occupant who also started to snack on the contents. They then moved off, heading downhill towards the town centre but this time at a leisurely pace that she could cope with, despite the slight residual discomfort in her foot. The gods were smiling on her at last! She sent a quick text message to keep Shazza informed then began the task of following them while trying to keep out of sight, just in case they turned round and spotted her. It was easier than she feared. The wheelchair duo were ambling along rather than stepping out quickly, just as if they were in no hurry. All the better for her. The doctor had advised her not to walk too far or fast for a few days.

Phyllis judged her pace well, maintaining a steady distance between her and the pair in front, and using her stick as a support. Not that she really needed it now. The pain in her toe had just about disappeared. She peered ahead. They were approaching the seafront. What would the boys do now? She had no idea where any of the youngsters lived or even why they'd decided to take an interest in that nuisance tramp. One of them had looked vaguely familiar, though. Shazza had said her name was Kerry and that she needed to be treated with caution. And the fact that they seemed to know someone from the police was a real concern. It meant that she and Shazza had to be doubly careful in everything they did. And, let's face it, Shazza wasn't the brightest spark in the box. She was likely to act first and think later. Or not think at all.

The wind was gustier here, with a stiff breeze blowing in from the bay. The black boy was now pushing the wheelchair along the separate promenade path, heading past the Pier Bandstand. Phyllis dropped back because it would be easier for one of the boys to spot her here if they were to turn around. They didn't though. She'd been concerned earlier about these teenagers being a bit clever and managing to discover some clues about what was going on. But there wasn't any need for her to worry, not on this evidence. The boys were heading towards a shelter on the promenade. Maybe the boy in the wheelchair was getting cold and needed to get out of the wind for a spell. She moved behind the war memorial so she couldn't be seen and phoned Shazza, informing her where she was and to get here, with Tommo, right now. The pair of them couldn't be far away. It was a good fifteen minutes since she'd texted them outside the hospital.

It was less than five minutes before Shazza and Tommo appeared.

'Wassup?' Shazza said. Phyllis wasn't sure how old Shazza was. She looked about eighteen but could have been a year or two older, or even younger. She was heavily built, had a mean look about her, was hot tempered and had a habit of suddenly lashing out in a rage if things didn't seem to be going her way.

'They're along in that shelter, Shazza,' Phyllis answered. 'The one in the wheelchair and the blackie one. I'm gonna confront them and ask them what they're up to. Mebbe put the frighteners on them. There's only two of them and the one in a wheelchair can't do nothin' much, can he? What d'you think, Tommo?'

Tommo bunched his fists and smirked. 'Could land a few if you want. Might keep them from doing any more snooping where they're not wanted.'

The problem with Tommo was that he really fancied himself as a hard man, like in the old gangster movies. He wanted to be tough, violent and ruthless. In reality he was none of these things. He was thin and bony, with a pinched appearance that made him look severely malnourished. The other problem was that he lacked any sense of judgement. Phyllis sometimes thought he lived in a parallel universe.

'Tell you what,' Shazza added. 'We can sit on either side so they can't get away. You can stand in front and have your say.'

Phyllis nodded. 'Good plan. But no punching, either of you, not unless I give the word. We don't want them getting even more cops involved. We gotta tread careful, like. We just wanna warn them off, stop them from poking their noses in again.'

The three of them walked around the corner of the shelter. Sure enough, the two teenage boys were sitting in the shelter, facing out to sea. They looked at the approaching trio. The lad in the wheelchair smiled at them.

'Hello,' he said. 'It took you longer than we thought to get here. What kept you?'

Phyllis stopped. What did he mean by that? She frowned in puzzlement and was about to put a hand on the arms of her two helpers to hold them back. Too late. They were too intent on causing trouble and hadn't spotted the challenge in the words the wheelchair boy had spoken. Shazza and Tommo had already sat down and were both gloating over what seemed to be a couple of easy targets. Phyllis heard a noise behind her and turned around.

The other five members of the Misfits were standing behind her. Rowan moved to sit beside a shocked-looking Shazza. Lee and Danny moved to the bench beside Tommo and sat down. Kerry and Fatima stood either side of Phyllis. They all looked serious and determined.

'What are you up to, Phyllis Prince?' Kerry asked.

Phyllis's jaw dropped. 'How do you know my name?' she spluttered.

'Oh, we know lots of stuff,' Kerry replied. 'We keep our eyes and ears open. So we know these two are called Shazza and Tommo. Now tell us what this is all about. We've got plenty of time. Do you want to sit down and take the weight off your feet? We don't want your injured toe to get any worse.'

Chapter 15: Emergency Session

The Misfits held an emergency session in the community centre that evening to discuss the day's events. It had been such an incident-packed time, full of ups and downs, discoveries and confrontations. They needed to get the events out in the open in order to discuss them before planning their next move. The problem, as Fatima explained to them all, was that they'd made a lot of progress but there was still no news of Daisy. And that was the whole purpose of their investigation. The trio down at the seafront, Phyllis, Shazza and Tommo, had owned up to being the people who had bullied and punched Daisy early in the week but denied doing anything else to her. They said that she'd been gone when they went back the next morning, which was exactly what Rowan had reported too.

'Do we believe them? That's the point. 'Cos if they're telling the truth, there's got to be another explanation for Daisy disappearing,' Fatima said.

'Yeah, but what other reason could there be?' Lee asked.

Kerry joined in. 'Lots, actually, Lee. We talked about it earlier in the week. The thing is, I sort of half-believe the three of them. They're idiots, really, trying to sell pills and junk in that small park and making it as obvious as they do. Real dealers used to use that place. What if they come back and find those three around? They'll make mincemeat of them.'

'It's not our problem, is it?' Rowan said. 'If they've got a death wish, that's up to them. They're the ones we saw on Monday night, and Shazza was the one who kicked Daisy. She half owned up to it.'

'She's the type,' Kerry added. 'I sort of vaguely knew her a couple of years ago when I used to hang around down in the town at night. She was sometimes there but kind of stayed on the fringe. She's a typical bully. Stays back from any trouble unless it's someone smaller or weaker than her, then she gets involved.'

'A bit like Blagger Banks, then,' Lee added.

'Yeah, I guess so. Did you ever get any more hassle from him, Lee?'

Lee shook his head. 'No. Thanks, Kerry. And I don't think he picked on anyone else either, not before we finished for half-term. It was only a few days, mind.'

Rowan broke in. 'But do bully's ever change? Can you see that Shazza ever being nice to anyone? You know, the way she looks at you when you're talking to her. Kind of sly, as if she's looking for a weakness. She'll always be like that, won't she?'

'We're not experts, Rowan,' Fatima said. 'Maybe someone like Rae might know more. But I like to think that people can change, given the right chances and the right advice. Maybe I'm being stupid thinking that, though, considering what's going on back in my own country. They're bullies with tanks and bombs, and don't care what they do and who they kill. Sometimes I think it's all too complicated.'

She frowned and fell silent. The others all knew about the deaths of her father and other close family members. They too fell silent. What could they say to her? What could anyone possibly say to a teenager whose father and younger sister had been deliberately murdered by their own government back in Syria?

Fatima suddenly spoke again. 'Cheer up, everyone. You're all too quiet. Let's have some choccie biscuits.'

At the mention of chocolate biscuits, Wolfie sped out of the room, returning a few moments later with a closed plastic tub.

'From my mum,' he explained. 'Millionaire's shortbread. She's been busy baking this afternoon and sent these along. I left the tub out beside the coatrack.'

'And that reminds me,' Fatima went on. 'Do you all want to come round to mine for lunch tomorrow? Mum says it's okay and I can practise my cooking. It'll be a change from meeting in the café again. I can do kebabs and some dips.'

'Oh, I love you, Fatima Haddad,' Wolfie said, mournfully. 'You've stolen my heart.'

'Get real, idiot,' she replied. 'You haven't tasted it yet.'

* * *

'Whaddya mean, it was a bunch of teenagers? Are you kidding me?' Gobbie had a face like thunder. He grabbed Phyllis Prince by the arm. 'We only just done this deal, just a coupl'a weeks ago. Are you tellin' me it's buggered up already? That ain't right.' He shook his head, clearly furious. 'Get it sorted, you stupid moron. I don't care how, just do it. We can't have a bunch of kids gettin' in the way.'

Phyllis swallowed hard. She felt as if she was trapped in a corner with no way out. 'Shazza said you might think of something else.'

'Are you crazy? Do you think I'd listen to my own stupid daughter's advice? She's never had any brains, not since the day she was born. The best thing you can do about anythin' Shazza says is to forget it. I don't even listen to her in the first place. It's a total waste o' time. If these other kids she told me about have even got twice her brains, they'll still be a total walkover. Just get it sorted.'

He turned and walked away into the darkness, leaving Phyllis staring, open mouthed. She felt a mixture of rage and hopelessness. She felt like kicking something but refrained. Injuring her toe the last time she'd acted on that impulse was lesson enough. What did he want from her? He seemed to think she could single-handedly outwit that group of seven teenagers. The only people she had to call on for help were Shazza and Tommo, neither noted for their high levels of intelligence and insight. Things didn't look good. Phyllis still didn't understand how the teenagers had managed to turn the tables on her. She turned around and hobbled back home. Her head ached from the effort of trying to understand what had gone wrong and her toe was throbbing again.

Chapter 16: At the Fort

There were lamb kebabs, chicken kebabs and vegetable kebabs, together with a selection of salads, dips, hummus and pitta, all set out across the table. Rowan suspected that Fatima and her brother Miran had spent much of the morning preparing and cooking the food. It looked delicious.

'Grab some while it's hot,' Fatima said. 'The plates are on the side over there.'

Plates and forks were passed around and the youngsters dug into the dishes in front of them. For a while the only sounds were noises of appreciation.

'Wow,' Wolfie said. 'This is totally yummy. I love you even more than I said yesterday, Fatima.'

'We love food,' Fatima said. 'Most Syrian people do. This is all healthy stuff. We can talk while we eat.'

'Yum. I might get the recipe for this chicken, Fatima,' Rowan said. 'I like to give my mum a rest from doing all the cooking and they'd like this. Most oldies don't like curries and spicy food, but my mum and dad do as long as it isn't too hot. And this isn't.'

'We don't use a lot of chilli,' Fatima replied. 'It's other spices like cinnamon, cloves and cumin. And sometimes paprika and sumac. Miran did the chicken one, didn't you, Miran? It's great.'

Miran smiled cheekily, picked up his plate and left the room, heading for the sitting room.

'I've got to look after Miran today,' Fatima went on. 'But Mum should be home by four. Either I've got to stay in or he comes with me, if I go out. Sorry.'

'That doesn't worry us. He's, what, ten?' Kerry said.

'Yeah. He's pretty sharp. Picks up on things quick. He's really at good spotting wildlife. Birds and stuff. He's in the dolphin watching group and goes out in the bay with them, in a neighbour's boat.'

'We've still got to decide on our next move.' Rowan said. 'Kerry, Danny and I were talking about it on our way here. We still think it's worth trying to find Gobbie and keep an eye on him. He knows something about Daisy but clammed up yesterday and went off in a huff.'

'Me and Fatima were gonna look for him yesterday afternoon,' Danny said, wiping a piece of pitta bread around his plate to mop up all the juices. 'But then those racist men had a go at her, and we got stuck with the police and that stuff. We never got to ask about Daisy at the station either. Maybe we should go back.'

Fatima bit her lip. 'I can't do that if I've got Miran with me. Mum would do her head in if she found out that I'd taken him with me, trying to find a nasty racist.'

'Wolfie and I can look after him,' Josh said. 'We can take him down to the front and do a dolphin watch. All these people talk about the dolphin pod that lives in the bay, but I've never seen them.'

'Yeah, we can go to the old fort, above the harbour entrance. You can see for miles from there,' Wolfie added. 'Got any binoculars?'

'Miran's got two sets,' Fatima replied.

'That's okay then. We'll look after Miran for the next couple of hours.'

Fatima laughed. 'You might have the wrong angle, you two. I bet it ends up with Miran looking after you. Good luck!'

'In that case, me, Kerry and Lee can go to the train station and ask if anyone remembers seeing Daisy,' Rowan said. 'The five of us can head off together, then split up near the station. Okay everyone? And remember to make a note of anything interesting. I don't wanna be too late back, though. Kerry and me, we're going clubbing tonight. It's Friday, our night out in the town.'

'Does that mean you'll be a bit hungover tomorrow morning?' Wolfie said, grinning as usual.

'I'm not gonna commit myself either way,' Rowan replied.

They helped to tidy the kitchen, made their way to the front door and separated. Josh was pushing Wolfie's wheelchair with Miran tagging along beside him and they turned west. The others headed east, towards the railway station.

As usual, Wolfie spent much of the time looking around him, observing people and the way they interacted. After all, what else was there for him to do, confined in a wheelchair the way he was? Josh and Miran chatted to each other about the wildlife that could be spotted around Weymouth. It wasn't just the dolphins that were of interest. Seals were sometimes seen in the area, along with a huge variety of seabirds. Miran was fascinated by the sea, even though it was chilly and grey for much of the year. The Haddad family had lived in the Aleppo region in Syria, far from the

Mediterranean. He told Wolfie that the area was often hot and dusty, made worse once the shelling and bombing started. There were clouds of dust everywhere and the smell of death hung in the air. Here the air was clean and fresh, even on a cool breezy October day like this.

They soon reached the harbour and crossed the river by the Town Bridge, then made their way along Nothe Parade towards the old fort that, at one time, guarded the entrance to the harbour. It was now a place of peace and tranquillity, with grassy areas, benches and viewpoints. Miran directed them towards his favourite lookout position.

'It was here I saw the dolphins,' he said, peering out above the retaining wall. He took out his binoculars and searched the water in front of him.

Wolfie found it difficult to see above the old ramparts from his position in his chair. He had Miran's older set of binoculars around his neck, but soon lost interest in the limited view available to him.

'You stay here,' he said. 'I'm just going to trundle around a bit, past the museum entrance into the gardens.'

He reassured the other two that he'd be fine and set off. He was enjoying being out in the fresh air and liked to be alone some of the time. It gave him an opportunity to use his arms to propel himself along, something that made him feel more independent. It was always good of people to push his chair so much, but he hated to feel reliant on others. He might be disabled but he wasn't helpless! He made his way further west along the network of paths that criss-crossed the area around the old fort. There was no danger of getting lost, not with the vast arc of Weymouth Bay so prominent on his left side and the Isle of Portland visible ahead, along with parts of the causeway.

He rounded a corner, heading towards a row of bench seats situated below a line of shrubs that acted as a windbreak, but then slowed from his previous fast pace. Two people were sitting on one of the benches, huddled up as a protection from the breeze. They had the look of homelessness about them, grizzled and weather-beaten, with threadbare clothes. The woman was wearing an extremely faded red beret. Weren't they the duo that Josh had said he'd spoken to in the library the day before? They certainly fitted his description. Wolfie wondered about returning to Josh and telling him but was worried that they'd be gone by the time he got back. He decided to approach them and have a chat, but first he checked the immediate area. There were other people about and the spot could be seen from the café. He should be safe enough. He also checked that his mobile phone was ready to use in a hurry. No point in ignoring the instructions from his parents. They had his best interests at heart, after all.

He brought his wheelchair to a halt beside them. He realised they'd been watching him.

'Hi,' he said. 'I'm Wolfie. I think my mate Josh had a chat with you in the library yesterday about someone who's gone missing. That's if you are Bets and Charlie.'

The half-interested way they'd been watching him altered as soon as they heard him mention the names. They stiffened noticeably.

'What if we are?' the man said, gruffly. He kept his hands in the pockets of his shabby raincoat and stared at Wolfie.

'Well, Josh probably told you. We're worried about Daisy Shaw. She got beaten up and she's gone missing. We want to find her and check that she's okay. Josh said that you might know her.'

The woman coughed throatily. 'Yeah, we do. But we ain't seen her this week.' She paused and looked at Wolfie carefully before going on. 'She's a good un, is Daisy. We're a bit worried about her too. We bin talkin' about her since yesterday, ain't we, Charlie? It'd be good if we knew where she was an' if she was okay, like.'

Charlie nodded.

Wolfie wondered about going for Josh and Miran, but they'd promised Fatima that they'd avoid involving the young boy in any investigation. He really didn't want to upset Fatima and lose her as a friend. He took out his notebook and pen and tried to smile at the couple.

'Can you tell me a bit about Daisy? I'll only jot down a few facts to jog my memory. It isn't very good.'

'What makes you think ours is any better?' Charlie commented.

Wolfie remembered something Rowan had said. 'We can only do the best we can,' he replied.

The couple nodded. 'We've known her a good few months, haven't we, Bets?' Charlie said. 'She's a local gal, from one of the villages. She started drinkin' heavy after her bloke went off with another woman. Then she lost her job 'cos of it. She got chucked out of her home when she couldn't pay the rent. That's just like a lot of us, going all downhill, like.'

'That's great to know,' Wolfie said. 'Have you been able to think of where she might have gone? If she was in trouble, I mean? We wonder if she's headed off somewhere where she feels safe. We just want to check she's okay, really.'

They both shook their head. 'Nah.'

Wolfie thought hard. 'Did she ever say what village she came from?'

Bets spoke up. 'I think it was Osmington. Not very far, anyway.'

'If we wanted to find you again, where would be the best place? We won't spread it about or anything. Honest.'

'We don't use the Market area much 'cos Gobbie's started hanging out there, and he's trouble,' Bets replied. 'We flit between the library area, the front and here. Bit windy up here in winter though. We only come up here today 'cos the sun's out.'

'Thanks so much. You've been really helpful. If we do find her, I'll let you know.'

Wolfie made his way back to the other two, still at the viewpoint and peering out to sea through their binoculars. He gave a thumbs up sign to Josh and mouthed that he'd tell him about it later.

Chapter 17: Gobbie

Fatima felt a kind of kinship with Danny and Kerry, although she'd never broached the subject of their parents' death with them. She'd picked up early on that their feelings about the loss of their parents had been very different to her own, concerning the killing of her father in Syria. That loss was like a gaping wound in her existence, raw and weeping like an ulcer. Kerry and Danny had lost their mum and dad in an arson attack on their house, but they'd been badly treated, maybe even abused, so probably didn't feel the same way about their parents as she and Miran did.

'Your Gramps is nice,' she said to Danny as they left the rest of the group near the station. 'I've had a chat with him at the community centre. You're lucky to have someone like him to look after you. He seems very caring.'

'Yeah,' Danny said. 'He's always been good. He talks to me about my future. I used to want to be a journalist and that's what he still thinks but I'm not so sure now. I feel awkward around other people and that's not good, is it? You've gotta be able to talk to people and think about what they're saying. I'd get too panicky. Science is my best subject at school so I might do that. See, you'd be a good journalist 'cos you're really good with words and you're a good planner.'

'Well, I'll have to see. Maybe I only wanted to be one 'cos of my dad, but he was a campaigning sort of person. Really, he should have been in politics but that just doesn't happen in Syria, not unless you're a government lackey. I wonder about studying law or even being a doctor, like my mum.'

They reached the footbridge over the railway, the spot they'd hoped to investigate the previous day, before they'd been delayed by the racist comments. The bridge itself was deserted but the park at the far side seemed to have people in it.

'You know what this man Gobbie looks like, don't you?'

'Yeah, I think so. He used to come round our house. He was a mate of Dad's. I didn't like him. I didn't like any of Dad's friends, they were drunk too much. They were horrible. Kerry didn't like them either. They used to be really rude to her. You know. Dirty, like. Suggestive.'

'I can guess. When I was back in Syria, I always thought Britain would be such a civilised sort of place, with people who were full of knowledge, because of Shakespeare and Winston Churchill and Florence Nightingale. But a lot of people aren't, are they? They can be just as nasty as anywhere else, though they haven't got guns and bombs and stuff like that. So they just make nasty comments instead. I think my dad knew that, but I didn't really listen to him as much as I should have.' She stopped suddenly a few yards into the park. 'Do you think that might be them over there, down at the town end? Let's just walk down and pretend we haven't seen them.'

Fatima and Danny took a path on the railway line side and followed it as it turned on itself, heading back north again but this time closer to the bench seats where the small group of down-and-outs were congregated. A large, scruffy dog growled softly and continuously as they approached.

'Quiet, Skipper,' one of the men said.

Fatima felt Danny flinch beside her. She looked at him and saw he was shaking.

'Are you alright, Danny?' she said quietly.

He shook his head. 'I wanna get away. Please.' He was almost pleading.

They hurried past the group of men, giving them a wide berth, and didn't stop until they were nearly fifty yards further on.

'What was the matter?'

'That dog. He called it Skipper. It's Tonto Leary's dog, the man who set fire to our house. He killed people.'

'Fatima looked at him incredulously. 'Was that him? Why is he still out of prison?'

'No, that's not him. He's locked away for life. But that's his dog. I hated it when he came round to see Dad. The dog would lie on the floor looking at me, growling all the time, as if it wanted to rip my throat out. I thought it was put down when he went into prison.'

'Was Gobbie there? Did you see him?'

'Yeah. He was the man who had the dog.'

'Do you want to sit down?'

Danny nodded so they walked on a few more yards to a bench that was in a sunny spot and sat down. Fatima took a water bottle out of her bag and offered it to Danny. He took a big swig.

'Maybe we shouldn't have come. I was a bit worried 'cos you went really pale back there,' Fatima said.

'No. It was right to come. We found Gobbie but I forgot how nasty he is. Now I remember.'

Fatima was still worried. If Gobbie was as unpleasant as Danny and Kerry seemed to think, was it safe to keep him under tabs? Maybe they should just try to find out where he stayed but how could they do that? Kerry had already told them that Gobbie had a different attitude to all the other rough sleepers. Maybe he wasn't one himself, but just pretended to be.

* * *

Rowan, Kerry and Lee had spent almost an hour at the railway station, talking to anyone who looked as though they might work or spend time in the vicinity. Platform staff, ticket office personnel, taxi drivers, even the car-wash workers in the car park. Nobody could remember seeing Daisy or anyone matching her description. It was both disappointing and reassuring at the same time.

'It means she hasn't left the area, not unless she's walked or gone by car,' Rowan said. 'The bus people told us yesterday they hadn't seen her, and now the same here. That's gotta be good, hasn't it?'

Lee agreed. 'She won't have a car, will she? She's got no money being a dosser, so how could she afford one?'

Kerry stood thinking. 'So, she's either still in the town or somewhere nearby. Let's head back to Fatima's and see what the others have found out.'

The best news, of course, came from Josh and Wolfie, with their discovery that Daisy had a connection

104

with the village of Osmington, only five miles east, and with a bus every couple of hours. Plans were made for the next day and the group separated.

She didn't speak about her concerns, but Kerry was deeply troubled by the possibility that Gobbie was somehow involved. She might appear to be afraid of nothing and no one, but there were one or two people that she avoided like the plague because of past events. Gobbie Walsh was one of them.

Chapter 18: The Pony Shelter

The plans for the first part of Saturday morning did not go as well as hoped for. The group met at the bus station as arranged, but both Kerry and Rowan seemed tired and subdued. When questioned they said they'd had a great night of clubbing, but both agreed they could have easily slept until midday. With them preferring to take a backseat, it was left to Fatima, Josh and Lee to take the lead. Then the bus that turned up was an old one that didn't rise and fall to allow easy access for Wolfie in his wheelchair. Instead the driver was forced to use an internal ramp that should have been easy to flip up from the bus's floor. It was stuck and a supervisor had to be called to help free it. The other passengers grumbled long and hard about nuisance teenagers causing unnecessary delays until Kerry lost her temper, turned and snapped at them.

'Some of you'll be in wheelchairs soon. You'll change your minds then, I bet.'

The muttered complaints stopped, and the bus finally set off nearly ten minutes late.

This was followed by the fall of an unexpected shower of rain just as the group climbed off the bus in Osmington fifteen minutes later. The driver got wet connecting and disconnecting the wheelchair ramp and was clearly displeased. By the time the gang had extracted waterproofs from their assorted backpacks they were already damp, and, to add insult to injury, the rain stopped just as the last hood was pulled up.

The sun even beamed down for a few seconds from a clear patch between the clouds.

Wolfie groaned as he unzipped his jacket. 'It's gonna be one of those days. I can feel it in my bones. Where are we going?'

Fatima checked her notebook. 'According to the phone book, there's a house up in Hillside Lane that's got someone called Shaw living in it. Bramble Cottage. I think it's left along there, beyond the village shop.'

They made their way up the narrow lane. It was lined by old houses and cottages, most with a garden. Lee, who sometimes helped his father in their own garden back in Weymouth, suspected the flower beds would look colourful on a sunny July day, although they looked less so today, dripping as they were with the residue of the recent downpour. Bramble Cottage was the last house on the left. Beyond it, the road surface became rougher, heading towards a cluster of farm buildings some two or three hundred yards further on. They stopped and looked. The small cottage was made of old grey stone and had a slate roof. Climbing roses grew around the front porch and a few late blooms still showed a dark pink coloration that brightened up the dreariness of the darkening, autumn leaves.

A woman came out of the neighbouring house and walked towards her car. She stopped when she saw them. Lee thought they'd better explain why they were there. He'd normally leave it to Kerry or Rowan but both of them still seemed half asleep.

''We're looking for someone called Shaw,' he explained. 'We're friends of a Daisy Shaw and we're trying to find her.'

'Oh, aye,' the woman replied. 'Daisy don't live here, not for years now. It's her brother, Roger, who's got this place, him and his family.'

'So you haven't seen Daisy recently?'

'No. It's all locked up, anyway. The family are away on holiday in Malta. They'll be back next Saturday.' She frowned. 'I shouldn't have told you that. It's all alarmed mind, and we've got neighbourhood watch around here.'

'It's okay,' Lee replied. 'We're not burglars or anything. We're worried about Daisy's health. We're volunteer helpers from the town.'

'Oh, I see. Well, as I said, I haven't seen her or anyone else.'

She gave them another suspicious look, got into her car and drove away.

'There are some sheds around the back,' Lee said. 'Maybe a couple of us should have a look.'

He, Fatima and Josh walked down the driveway to the back of the property. The rear garden had a lawn, several flower and herb beds, and vegetable patches. Fruit trees and shrubs meant that much of the garden couldn't be seen from neighbouring properties. There was a shed near to the house and a small paddock beyond the back garden with a solitary pony grazing peacefully. A neat, timber shelter was situated in the corner of the paddock and looked to be partly filled with straw. Lee looked around. Everything was so quiet, so peaceful. He felt Josh tap him on the arm. He was pointing to a plastic plate and cup laying on the ground near the cottage's back door, next to a water tap. They walked quietly over to have a closer look. There were crumbs and a bit of bread crust on the plate, soggy from the recent rain shower.

'That could be recent, like this morning,' Josh whispered. 'There might be someone here but not in the house.'

Fatima also spoke. 'That pony shelter in the paddock might be just the place for someone trying to hide, someone who was used to sleeping outside. It's got straw in it.'

They returned to the front of the property as quietly as possible and told the others of their suspicions.

'We can't all go,' Lee said. 'If she's there, she'll be scared. Best if it's just three of us.'

Rowan spoke. 'Why don't you three go back? You've seen it and know where you're going. And you're younger than Kerry and me. You'll be less threatening if she's there. Agreed, everyone?'

The trio returned to the back garden and made their way down the path and through the back gate into the field. They approached the timber shelter and Fatima peered inside. There was a rustling sound from the pile of straw in the corner and a grubby, frightened face peeked out at them.

'Daisy!' Fatima said.

Daisy looked terrified. She put her hand to her mouth and crawled away, trying to hide behind the stack of straw bales. It was clear that she'd been

109

sleeping in the straw; a thick layer had been pulled out across the floor and the imprint of her body shape could be seen in the shallow pile. Daisy was clutching her right elbow, held up in a dirty sling made from a torn pink scarf.

'Don't be scared,' Fatima said. 'We're here to help. We've been looking for you. We've got you some food.'

The woman lowered her head and sank back onto a straw bale. She started to cry, huge racking sobs. Fatima turned to Lee and flicked her head, indicating that he should go for the others. She slowly approached Daisy.

'I'm only trying to help, Daisy. You really don't look well. What's happened to your arm?'

As she got closer, she could see several bruises on Daisy's arms and face. It hadn't been as bad as that on Monday night, surely? What had gone on between then and Tuesday morning when Rowan had noticed she was missing? Had someone attacked her?

'Daisy, I'm going to get my mum across here to take a look at you. She's a doctor. If someone's beaten you up, you might have a fracture or something even worse.'

'I don't wanna go to hospital,' Daisy whispered hoarsely, holding herself tight. 'I hate them places.'

She was still crying, but this time it sounded as if she was in pain. She suddenly lurched to one side and was sick on the floor. Not very much came up. It looked as though she'd eaten nothing else but a few bits of dry bread. Fatima became even more worried and quickly phone her mother. How unwell was Daisy?

Fatima's mother was with them within twenty minutes, wearing scrubs and carrying her medical bag. She hurried out of the car and followed Kerry through the garden and into the pony shelter.

'Where's Miran?' Fatima asked. She could tell by the look on her mother's face that she was displeased at being called out on what might be a wild goose chase.

'He's in the playroom at the clinic, and not very happy. He's twice the age of any other child there. This had better be worth it, Fatima.'

Fatima stepped back and pointed to the sick-looking Daisy, laying on the straw and breathing shallowly. Her mother frowned again and moved closer. She felt Daisy's forehead then used her stethoscope to check her ragged breathing. She then examined her abdomen and finally her arms and legs.

'You're forgiven,' she said to Fatima. 'This woman is seriously ill and needs to be in hospital for some further check-ups.' She held her hand up to cut short the protestations that started to come from the youngsters. 'I don't care what she said about not going into hospital. It's gone beyond that. I think she's got several broken ribs and may have internal injuries. Added to which she might have a fracture in her arm. She needs X-rays and a more detailed examination. If we don't get her into hospital she might die, so she's going in whether you like it or not. And that's all I have to say on the matter.'

She took her phone out and spoke for several minutes, then looked at her watch, shaking her head. She sighed. 'I've got to get back. I have a list of appointments that will now run late.'

111

'Sorry, mum,' Fatima said.

Her mother touched her cheek. 'No, you did the right thing. I'll have to go, though. Someone needs to wait out on the road for the ambulance.'

She scribbled a few notes on an official pad, tore the page out and handed it to Fatima. 'Give this to the medics who come. They'll be expecting it.'

She left after giving a wave and a thin smile. She looked harassed.

An ambulance arrived some ten minutes later. The paramedics read the slip, briefly examined Daisy, stretchered her into the ambulance and then set off for the county hospital, blue light flashing.

The group caught the next bus back to town and wondered about calling in to their favourite café for a celebration lunch. But in the end, they left the bus station feeling curiously downhearted, despite having achieved their objective of finding the missing outcast and doing their best to ensure she was safe. How ill was she? Had she been so seriously injured that her life was in danger? Clearly Fatima's mother had thought so, and she was a doctor. No one felt elated at the morning's events. Kerry and Rowan had planned for another night on the town but decided against it. Instead, they would try to find out if a visit to the County Hospital was possible. The trouble was it was twelve miles away in Dorchester.

'Can we all meet tomorrow morning?' Rowan said. 'But we need to find out if we can visit first. It might be family only.'

Fatima spoke up. 'That's what my mum said, that we wouldn't be allowed in to see her. She might be able to get us in to visit once Daisy comes back here to the local hospital to recuperate in a couple of days.'

'In that case, let's not meet 'til Monday. Kerry and me'll be back to normal then.' She laughed. 'Hopefully!'

'What time did you get in last night?' Fatima asked quietly, curious at the lack of verve from the two people who had set the group up and led it through its first few days.

'Three thirty,' Rowan whispered. 'I told my parents it was just after midnight and they believed me, I think. It was just brill, Fatima. I never believed I could have that much fun. It's so great being a girl, but my feet and legs are sore from all that dancing. Listen, if you wanna come with us sometime, just tell me. We're gonna do it again next week. Kerry wants to go out again tonight but I'm not sure. I haven't felt this tired for ages.'

Chapter 19: Sunshine

It was a sunny and bright Monday during the autumn half-term week, so there was an expectation around the town that crowds of tourists and day-trippers would flood the area. The cafes, ice-cream parlours and trinket shops were all open bright and early, hoping that one last week of tourist-based sales would get them through the long, quiet winter ahead. The town looked lovely, particularly the area around the promenade, with its lawns and flower beds. The Misfits were meeting in one such area, congregated around two bench seats in the beach gardens.

Kerry gazed out to sea. 'It's really warm today and the water's calm. How about swimming this afternoon?'

'Won't it be a bit cold?' Wolfie asked.

'Yeah, well, it'll be chillier than back in August or September, but warmer than May or early June. Would you be okay, Wolfie?'

'I think so. I'll check with Mum. I'll need a couple of people to help me, but water's good. It's the buoyancy. I can splosh around for a bit, no problem. Gotta watch the cold, though.'

Fatima chipped in. 'Daisy's not being moved down here to the local hospital 'til tomorrow, according to Mum. So we can't visit 'til Wednesday. Mum said she'll find a way of getting us in but only two or three of us. We'll need her help 'cos we're not family. So there's not much for us to do today.'

'I found out a bit more about Gobbie yesterday. He's living in the same flat as before, when he knew our Dad.

I went round to watch and saw him when he came out to put some rubbish in the bins,' Kerry said.

Josh was surprised. 'I thought he was homeless, like the others.'

She shook her head. 'Nah. Not Gobbie. He's a sly one. I dunno what he's up to and why he keeps mixing with Togs and the others. Do you think he might just be doing it to get information? It always looks as though he's listening to what everyone says. I never trusted him, never.'

'That's the problem,' Josh continued. 'We've found Daisy, but we still don't know why someone beat her up. If it was Gobbie or that odd woman Phyllis, or even that Shazza or Tommo, why did they do it? I'm pretty sure it was Shazza and Tommo that were there Monday night last week, when she was in the doorway. And it could have been Phyllis hanging back a bit. But why did someone go back and give her a real going over? It was a lot nastier than earlier.'

'Yeah, and how did she get to that place in Osmington?' Lee asked. 'I've been thinking about that since Saturday. She didn't get a bus 'cos we checked at the bus station. She couldn't have walked there, not in the state she was in. So how? That's what I'd like to know.'

Danny spoke up. 'The police are on it now. Rae, our detective friend, came to see us yesterday and she says it's a serious assault. And guess what? She's taking charge. But we're not allowed to do any more checking up. She says it might be dangerous.'

They all looked glum. It was due to their efforts that the badly injured woman had been found. Surely they weren't being excluded now?

Fatima spoke up. 'She's got to say that. If she didn't warn us off, she wouldn't be doing her job and she might get into trouble. It's the same with my mum. People in an official position of some kind have to follow those kinds of rules or they might lose their jobs. Or people might even sue them to get money. But we can sort of ignore the warning a bit. You know, keep our eyes open but be really careful. Like you, Kerry, yesterday afternoon, finding Gobbie. We can just watch and listen. If we're in the right place, we might discover something.'

Wolfie chipped in. 'Yeah, you're right. Anyway, I've gotta go and find Bets and Charlie, the two I saw at the Fort on Friday. I said I'd let them know if we found Daisy. They're pally with her. They might be able to tell us a bit more.'

'What, you mean they know more than they've let on?' Lee said.

'Yeah. All these people are really secretive. Maybe they're all scared. Whatever it is, they clam up all the time and only let teeny-weeny bits of information out. So why don't we do it now? Me, Josh and Danny. They saw them first in the library, and me at the fort. They know us. They might be around here somewhere. They said they use the library if it's cold, but here and the fort if it's sunny.'

'Great idea,' Kerry said. 'The rest of us can find out a bit more about those two pricks, Shazza and Tommo. I bet they know a bit about what's going on. Let's meet back here at lunchtime. Bring some food and your swimming stuff. Okay? Listen. Rae, the detective, is in town this afternoon. Shall I tell her we'll be on the beach in case she wants to see us?'

'Yeah. Maybe she'll give us an update. Maybe she's already found out who done it,' Rowan said.

* * *

Danny was the youngest member of the group and the quietest. His Asperger's meant he really had to force himself to speak up in a group, when it was much easier just to stay quiet and keep his awkwardness hidden. But he could relax a bit when there were only three of them together, and Wolfie was such an extrovert that Danny couldn't help but laugh at some of the things he said and did. There was one advantage to joining in less than the others, though. He spotted things that they might miss. And it happened again right now, on the promenade. Wolfie and Josh were larking about around the outside of the flower beds, with Josh pushing the wheelchair as fast as he could, then swerving around corners. Danny was trying to keep up but was also keeping his eyes peeled. There were a couple of people sitting on a bench seat with their backs to the trio. Could it be the two they were seeking? Danny took a side path that gave him a better view. It looked like them. He chased after the wheelchair duo and told them to switch direction. They turned and finally screeched to a halt in front of the seated pair. It was Bets and Charlie, as Danny had thought. He wondered if they'd been dozing in the sunshine because

117

they were looking a bit sleepy, but maybe they always looked like that.

Wolfie lost no time in speaking up. 'Hi there. It's us again and we've got good news. Well, good and not so good. We found Daisy on Saturday, out at Osmington. But she's had to go to hospital 'cos of her injuries. Someone beat her up really bad. But she's getting better, so that's good, isn't it?'

Bets finally spoke. 'Well, it's good to know she'll be okay. I 'spect the cops'll be round the place now, will they? Or won't they bother 'cos she's homeless? We usually get totally ignored by everyone. They couldn't care less about us.'

'No, there's an investigation with a proper detective. Daisy could've died.' Wolfie went quiet for a while.

Danny chipped in. 'Why would someone do that? Do you know? We can't understand it.'

Bets shrugged. 'Listen. Nasty stuff happens all the time to people like us. We just get used to it. It's good you got interested. Makes a change, I can tell you.'

Josh was more cautious than Wolfie. 'Maybe keep quiet about it, yeah? Someone did all that to her, prob'ly to scare her away. The police are trying to find out who, so we shouldn't give them a warning.'

Charlie eyed him carefully. 'Right. Anyways, we justs wanna quiet life, left alone. We don't wanna get involved in any trouble, do we, Bets?'

'Nah. We just wanna slide through life wiv no friction. I loves it when the weather's like this. Outside, in the sun. Can't be beat. Don't want no trouble.'

118

Danny frowned. This wasn't right, this outlook on life. It sounded good, but if the Misfits hadn't found Daisy when they did, she might have died. And would any of these people have known? Would they have even missed her? They wouldn't have bothered looking for her, that was for sure. They weren't bad people. Well, apart from Gobbie. He was a thug, just the type who'd beat someone up 'til they almost died. But they weren't good either. They didn't seem to want to lift a finger to help anyone else. Danny couldn't understand that attitude. Surely everyone ought to help others? Then he thought of what his own father had been like and realised not everyone put kindness first. Some people just seemed to turn out selfish and bad. Was it all down to bad luck? He knew Gramps had said he'd got to Kerry just in time. Any longer doing the kind of things she'd been involved with and it would've been too late for her. She'd have become a drunken, druggie slut, though Gramps didn't use those words. But Danny knew what he meant.

He looked at the other two. 'Maybe we should go,' he said. He didn't want them to say too much.

They turned and headed back to the town centre.

* * *

So who exactly were Shazza and Tommo, the teenagers who'd given Daisy a hard time the previous week and who'd also been involved in that confrontation in the shelter on Thursday afternoon? Kerry had recognised Shazza from a year or two earlier, when she herself had run wild for a while. That's when she'd been named Mad Kerry Fenners, gaining fame for

119

her willingness to do anything and try anything, all in an attempt to escape the misery of her life at home. That episode in her life had been brought to a shuddering halt by the death of her parents, then the move to live with Gramps and the subsequent friendship she'd formed with Rae Gregson, the detective. Shazza had been on the fringes of that loose-knit group of teenagers who'd hung around areas of the town centre at night to drink cheap booze and wait to see what Mad Kerry would get up to.

No-one else from the Misfits recognised her, so she wasn't a pupil at any of their schools. Kerry and Rowan didn't think she was at the local sixth form college either. Maybe she was a year or two older than them and worked somewhere. Maybe she didn't work but just hung around all day. Was her friend Tommo the same? Not even Kerry had recognised him. Yet Weymouth wasn't a big town, and a lot of the local youngsters knew each other, even if it was only slightly. Maybe he'd only moved here recently, or he was from somewhere else nearby.

Lee spoke up. 'The only one we know the last name of is that woman, Phyllis Prince. It's a lot easier finding someone if you know their surname. I don't think we're gonna get anywhere finding Shazza and Tommo 'til we find their surnames. I reckon she lives local so why don't we find out a bit more about her? Maybe a phone book or something? Or could we just ask around?'

Fatima frowned and looked worried. 'If we start asking people if they know her, it might get back to her. Do you remember how shocked she was when we used her name and told her we knew about her broken toe? She probably thinks we know all about her already and that's good, isn't it? Whereas all we really know is her name because Josh overheard her at the hospital. We should only ask around as a last resort. We need to be clever and find out about her in a really sneaky way.'

'Well, we're all waiting, Fatima. What's the plan?' Kerry said.

Fatima shook her head miserably. 'I can't think of one, not right now. All this is so hard.'

'Let's go home to get our swimming and picnic stuff,' Rowan suggested. 'Maybe we'll think of something this afternoon.'

Chapter 20: On the Beach

Weymouth has a long beach with soft golden sand, and the Misfit members made the most of it. After a lunch in which they shared their food and drink, they had a game of three-against-four badminton with an imaginary net and a court drawn out as lines in the sand. The game ended in chaos, with Wolfie switching sides depending on how he felt at any given moment. It was time for the water!

Lee felt that it was noticeably chillier than when he'd been for a swim the previous month, but he knew from lessons at school that the seawater around Britain took a while to cool down after an August high. It was still warmer than in early June, as Kerry had said. October was probably the last month you could go in without a wetsuit. At least the air was warm, helped by the bright sunshine but, even so, they'd need to stay active and keep an eye on Wolfie in case he got too cold.

It was the first time they'd seen Wolfie out of his wheelchair. Josh and Kerry each took and arm and helped him into the water. There were few waves; the lack of any breeze had seen to that. Once he was in up to his chest he started to swim and seemed more at home in the water than anyone other than Rowan.

'I do loads of water therapy,' he said. 'I'm better in the water than I am on dry land. My therapist says I ought to have been a fish.'

'What type? A salmon or a swordfish?' Josh quipped.

'A minnow or a manta-ray?' This was Rowan taking up the challenge.

'A stickleback or a shark?' Kerry laughed, splashing water over Rowan and Josh.

'A goldfish or a gudgeon?' Danny added.

'Wow, Danny. That was quick thinking,' Kerry said.

'A haddock or a halibut?' Fatima said quickly, before she could be splashed.

Everyone looked at Lee, ready to soak him.

'Perch or pike!' he yelled trying to turn and distance himself from the group.

'Boring!' Josh shouted and started to splash Lee anyway, soon joined by the others. They then ducked below the surface for a short game of underwater handstands. Josh had brought a whistling beach bomb with him, so they separated into a large circle and spent time hurling it through the air. It wasn't just Wolfie who thought that it was the most fun he'd had for ages. The same was true for Fatima, Lee and Josh. They all made their way out of the sea after an hour and flung themselves onto the sand.

'That was brill,' Lee gasped. 'I'm worn out though.' He began to towel himself dry.

Fatima leaned across and started to tickle him.

'Aargh!' he shrieked. 'I wasn't expecting that. Unfair!'

The next ten minutes was spent in a mass tickling frenzy, with everyone chasing across the sand trying to tickle someone else, even Wolfie who'd returned to his wheelchair. Finally, they flopped back onto the sand, gasping and out of breath. They'd all lost any sense of chill they'd had on emerging from the water.

Wolfie reached into a pocket in the fabric of his chair, pulling out a banknote. 'The ice-creams are on me! Dad gave me some cash when he heard I was coming to the beach with you lot.'

There was a scramble towards the kiosk as they started to argue about their favourite flavours. They returned to their mound of backpacks and clothes to enjoy their ices.

Fatima licked at a lump of crystalline ginger in hers. 'I've got a sort of idea,' she said. 'We know Phyllis Prince isn't on any social media so we can't trace her that way. I've looked in the phone book and she isn't listed there. So we've got to be really sneaky about it. Maybe we should split up again. One group can go back to talk to the people who helped us when we were looking for Daisy. You know, Togs and Bets and Charlie. But do it cautiously so we don't give the game away. Then another group can go round some shops and places, like the post office. Maybe we can pretend we've found something of hers and want to return it. I know it's not much of an idea but it's the best I can do.' She looked glum.

Lee chipped in. 'Sounds good. But I've thought of something else. We're planning to visit Daisy Wednesday afternoon after she's been transferred here from the county hospital. Why don't we ask her? For all we know, she might have some idea why she was picked on.'

Rowan reached across and slapped him on the back. 'Yeah. That's so good, Lee. We've kind of assumed that she didn't know anything but that's not likely to be true, is it? Why can't we do it tomorrow?'

Fatima spoke. 'She's probably being bought down in an ambulance but I don't know when. That's what my mum said. They won't let her have any visitors 'til they check her out. Wednesday is the soonest we can get in. Even then, it'll only be two or three of us.'

'How's she getting on?' Rowan asked.

'Okay. If there was a problem, they'd keep her up in the big hospital. But she's improving. I think she's been getting the best food she's had for ages. That must make a difference. And she's warm. And clean.' The last phrase was added as an extra. They all now realised the almost impossible difficulties that rough sleepers faced in trying to keep themselves and their clothes clean.

'I'll ask my mum to keep us up to date.' Fatima added. 'She's asked for Daisy to be added to her own patient list. That means she's her GP.'

Kerry made a decision. 'We can follow up Fatima's ideas tomorrow, 'cos there's nothing else for us to do. Then three of us can go and visit Daisy on Wednesday. How does that sound?'

There was agreement all round and they settled back in the sunshine.

'Hi.'

They all looked up to see the tall figure of Rae Gregson approaching. 'Glad to see you're all out enjoying the beach.' She settled onto the sand beside them.

'Any news?' Kerry asked.

''I can't tell you anything, not about an ongoing investigation. Sorry. Thanks for the list of names, by the way. The trouble is, apart from Phyllis Prince, they're all nicknames. But we're doing what we can.'

'What about Phyllis Prince?' Kerry asked, looking hard at the detective. 'Don't we have a right to know? We gave you her name.'

Rae hesitated. 'Okay. We've interviewed her but she denies any involvement. There's no proof of anything, Kerry. And that's what we need.'

Kerry looked glum. 'Yeah, we knew it would be hard.'

'But what I do want to say is that you must all stay away from that Gobbie, or whatever his real name is. We've managed to identify him and we're slowly building up a picture, though we haven't got there yet. But a few other people have told us about him. He's clearly not a nice person and I don't want any of you getting hurt. Understood?'

They all nodded and agreed.

'I guess I'm too late to join you in the water, by the looks of things. But does anyone fancy another swim? I've got my costume on under this lot.'

Rowan was up like a shot. 'Yeah, me! I'd love to. We were just mucking around earlier, and I fancy a proper swim.'

Like the others, Rowan was still wrapped in her towel. She dropped it to reveal her swimsuit, in a blue and white polka-dot pattern with a short skirt attachment. She watched as Rae slid out of her jeans and top, revealing a figure-hugging swimsuit in a brightly coloured flower pattern. It made the most of her small bust and created an eye-catching cleavage.

'I'm so jealous of you, Rae,' Rowan said as they walked to the water's edge. 'You've got a great figure.'

Rae turned and smiled. 'Listen, Rowan. You're fine. Don't expect too much in a hurry. You've got a wonderful shape and you're going to be a real beauty. Just don't rush it, okay?'

They trotted into the water, dived underneath a wave and swam out into deeper water, watched by the rest of the gang from their position on the beach.

'She's just the best thing for Rowan,' Kerry said. 'Imagine having no one to look up to for ages and then Rae appearing. Look at them. Rowan just idolises her. It's obvious.' She turned to face the others. 'Isn't this all going great? I don't mean us trying to find what happened to Daisy. I mean, just us, together like this. When Rowan and me got the idea for the group, we never thought it would be as good as this. I'm so full of buzz about it. It's really cool to be together like we are.'

Lee responded. 'Yeah. It's just so good. I feel better than I have for years. About myself, I mean. I guess we all do. Thanks, Kerry. You did all this.'

Chapter 21: The Searchers

Tuesday dawned dull and drizzly, not the ideal weather conditions for their plan of splitting into groups to track down Phyllis Prince. Luckily, by the time they met mid-morning, the drizzle had largely gone but the sky was still overcast, and a mist hung over the nearby high ground.

'Good job we managed to get to the beach yesterday,' Wolfie said. 'That might have been our last chance for a swim this year. Kerry, you're a genius for thinking of it.'

Kerry laughed. 'That's the first time I've ever been called a genius. Probably the last too. Wolfie, you're a real smoothie.'

Danny was watching his sister with a feeling of pride. He knew how much some of the adults in their family had given up on Kerry, only a year or two earlier, along with most of her teachers. Now look at her. It was like one of his own teachers had told him the previous year. People can sometimes change when they're given a chance. That was so true of his sister. She'd blossomed since they'd been living with Gramps and she'd started at the college.

'Can I go to the post office to ask about that Phyllis Prince?' he said. 'I know one of the shop ladies there. She lives along the road from us. Do you want to come too, Lee?'

'Yeah, of course.'

Kerry spoke up. 'The rest of us can split into two groups. So where should we try? Who's got some ideas?

Togs and Toast might know somethin', and they're okay. They won't snitch on us. What about the other two, Bets and Charlie, like Fatima suggested yesterday? D'you think they'd want to see us again? Won't they be getting fed up with us?'

Wolfie grinned. 'Nah. They like me. I've won 'em over. Leave 'em to me. They're like putty in my hands.'

'Wolfie, you talk total nonsense,' Fatima laughed.

'Yeah, but look where it gets me. Mum reckons I could talk my way into the Ritz for a free meal. No, seriously. People take pity on me and tell me all kinds of things. Then there are those who think I must be doolally because I'm a kid in a wheelchair. So they talk to each other about all kinds of stuff, thinking I'm stupid and can't understand what they're saying. I find out lots of gossip that way. Did you know one of the town councillors is having it off with his next-door neighbour? I learned that in the queue at the corner shop. These two people were whispering to each other about it and checking that no-one could overhear them, but they ignored me completely, and I was right in front of them. They claimed he wears bright yellow underpants. The councillor, I mean.'

'My dad's a councillor,' Rowan said.

There was a sudden silence, and everyone looked horrified.

'Only joking,' Rowan laughed. 'Got you there, didn't I?'

* * *

Danny and Lee set out for the town's main post office and spent much of the time chatting about their saxophone lessons. Both of them played alto sax in the local junior wind band. Although they went to different schools, they had the same saxophone teacher and she'd encouraged them both to go to Saturday morning rehearsals. The band practised for an hour and played a concert at the end of each term, held either in the town's Pavilion Theatre or in the Old Town Hall. The audience was mainly made up of parents and friends but taking part had improved Danny's self-confidence. It was so different, playing music. It didn't have all the stresses of conversation, in trying to understand what people meant by the things they said. Music was music: you just read the music and then got on and played it. A lot of the tunes they played were good fun. Jazz stuff, blues and even fast rock songs. Some of it was hard and they made mistakes, but no one seemed to mind much. At the concerts, the mums and dads just clapped along anyway.

They reached the post office and went inside. It wasn't very busy, just a group of elderly people collecting their pensions and a lady sending some parcels to Australia. Danny joined her queue. Lee guessed that the counter assistant was the one he wanted to speak to.

'Hello, Danny,' the lady behind the desk said when they reached the counter. 'We don't see you in here very often.'

'No, Mrs Bennett. I'm in for a special reason today, trying to find someone. I've gotta find out where Phyllis Prince lives. Can you help?'

'Why's that? Why do you need to find her address?'

Lee took over at this point, as they'd decided on the way here. Danny found it hard to deliberately deceive people and would often give the game away by fidgeting and looking embarrassed.

'We were on the beach yesterday and a lady was reading a book. She left it behind. Her name was in it but not her address, and we want to give it back to her.'

'Maybe she finished it and didn't want it any more.'

Lee tried to keep calm and think. 'No. There's a bookmark in it. She's only got halfway.'

Mrs Bennett turned to the other staff member. 'Do we know where a Phyllis Prince lives?'

The other lady shrugged. 'Somewhere up near the back of the hospital, I think. In a block of flats. Someone with that name was in last week with a complaint about a post delivery. I told her it was nothing to do with us and she'd have to go to the sorting office, but she wouldn't listen. A real pain.' She raised her eyebrows and pulled a face.

That sounded just the kind of thing their Phyllis Prince would do; make a complaint in the wrong place. Lee and Danny smiled politely at the two desk-staff.

'Thanks, Mrs Bennett. That's really helpful.'

The two boys waited until they were outside then high-fived each other.

'Wow. I never thought we'd find out about her so quick,' Lee said.

Danny felt really happy. He'd felt in awe of the others since they'd started this investigation a week earlier. The ideas and most of the discoveries had come from the other five. He and Lee had taken part in everything, but he felt they'd both been overshadowed. Not any longer.

They made their way back to their usual café, where they'd agreed to meet for lunch. Josh and Wolfie were already there, sitting in silence.

'Well, that was a waste of time,' Wolfie said. He looked despondent.

Josh chipped in. 'Yeah. Me and Wolfie got nowhere. We found Bets and Charlie, but they clammed up and wouldn't talk to us. They were in a really bad mood.'

They all ordered milk shakes to drink while they waited for the others. It wasn't long before the door opened, and the three girls came in. They looked quiet too.

'Someone's got to them,' Kerry said. 'Someone's put the frighteners on. Togs always chats to me, whenever we bump into each other. She's never ignored me like that.'

'We were the same,' Josh said. 'Our two were really moody. They told us to get lost.'

Wolfie was indignant. 'What kind of attitude is that? I mean, we found Daisy and got her to hospital. If it wasn't for us, she might be dead. Don't they realise that?'

Kerry scowled. 'Like I said, someone's scared them. Someone's told them not to talk to us. I bet it's that Gobbie. He's a nasty shit.'

'So we haven't got anywhere. We're stuck,' Rowan said.

Danny and Lee grinned.

'No we're not,' Lee said.

'We found out where she lives. Well, sort of. From the lady in the post office,' Danny added.

'Danny was brill. He started talking to her then I took over. It was just like we planned on the way there.'

'Yeah. We found she lives in a flat on a street round the back of the hospital.'

Lee continued. 'There are only a few blocks of flats near there. And my auntie lives in one of those streets. I can ask her.'

There were looks of relief on everyone's faces. Wolfie pulled another bank note out of his pocket. 'It's from my Dad again. He's so glad I've found you lot as friends. Pizza this time?'

The next ten minutes were spent choosing food from the café's menu and ordering. They settled down at their large table again and chatted while they waited for their lunches to arrive.

Rowan was the first to speak. 'We shouldn't go against what Rae told us. Not too much, anyway. She said we mustn't go looking for whoever it was that assaulted Daisy.'

Fatima was quick with her reply. 'We're not. We're trying to find Phyllis Prince and discover why she's so interested in us. It's totally different. That's what I think.'

'Yeah, but is it? Really, I mean? Isn't that just us being a bit devious? C'mon. We know it's all lumped together really.'

'Are you saying we should give up now that Daisy's been found?'

Rowan shook her head. 'Not really. I don't know what I'm saying. I'm a bit confused.'

Fatima kept going. 'The thing is, Rowan, this gives us a sense of purpose. It gives us a focus. If it weren't for this search, we'd just be a bunch of kids with nothing much to do. Wouldn't we just drift apart after a while? We're all different ages, with different interests. Okay, we all feel misfits in a way but is that enough to keep us together? I love the thought of us as a group of teenage investigators. It's what I've always wanted to do and here I am, doing it, for the first time in my life. I told you my dad was a journalist back in Syria and that's why he was killed. He never stopped. He went on finding things out and writing about them until the day they murdered him. And that's the way I feel. There's something odd going on. I want to know what. I like Rae but she's in the police. We'll never get told what's behind this, not by her or anyone else unless there's a court case and what chance is there of that? D'you really think Daisy's gonna press charges?' She shook her head. 'If we don't find out ourselves, we'll never know.'

The rest of the group were staring at her in awe. Kerry was the first to speak. 'Wow, Fatima. That was a heck of a speech. You're really passionate about it, aren't you?'

Rowan looked sheepish. 'You're right. I was just being a bit silly.'

Fatima answered. 'No, you weren't. We can see you really like Rae. And we like her too. But she's police so she's gotta give us those instructions. It's what I said yesterday.'

134

Josh spoke up. 'I'm with Fatima. We ought to have a purpose. What we're doing is totally right, and that's what the Misfits should be for. Finding things out and helping people in trouble.'

'How come you can speak as good as that, Fatima? Your English is better than any of the rest of us, and we're English!' Lee added.

Fatima looked sheepish. 'It was my dad. He taught me English from when I was tiny and made me read books, like Dickens and stuff. And he taught me how to debate. I've already got my GCSE English. I took it when I was twelve, back in Syria.'

The rest of the gang looked at her in astonishment. 'What grade did you get?' Lee asked.

Her answer came as a near whisper. 'Um, an A star.'

They all broke into applause. Then their food arrived.

'Let's get stuck in,' Kerry said. 'Then maybe we can give Lee's auntie a visit this afternoon.'

Chapter 22: Near Disaster

Lee rang the bell for his auntie's flat and waited. Only he and Fatima were here, on the doorstep. The rest of the group were outside, sitting on a bench near the lawn. The door opened and a tall blonde lady in a short dress peered out at them.

'Oh, it's you, Lee. I was expecting someone else.' She glanced at her watch, frowning.

'I don't need long, Auntie Bex. We're looking for someone and you might be able to help.'

'Well, you'd better come in. But I only have a couple of minutes.' She seemed slightly irritated.

Lee repeated the story he and Danny had told the staff at the post office.

Auntie Bex eyed the two youngsters suspiciously. 'I can't believe you're going to this much trouble over an old book.' She looked carefully at Fatima. 'And who are you?'

'I'm Fatima Haddad, Lee's friend.' Fatima decided not to elaborate.

Lee's aunt looked at her watch again. She clearly wanted to get rid of the two youngsters as quickly as possible. 'She lives downstairs, in one of the ground-floor flats. Number three, I think. I saw her going out about half an hour ago. She's a bit odd and keeps herself to herself. Look, I'd usually invite you in for some biscuits and a longer chat, Lee. But I can't today. Is that all you need?'

'Yeah,' Lee replied. 'Thanks. Maybe we'll see you soon.'

'Okay. Bye, Lee. Bye, Fatima.'

The two youngsters turned back to the stairwell and slowly descended.

'She's nice,' Fatima said.

'I think she's got a new boyfriend,' Lee replied. 'I heard Mum talking about it last week. Normally she chats a lot to me, but she looked like she was really disappointed when she saw it was us at the door. And I've never seen her in a dress before. She always wears jeans.'

Just as they reached the bottom of the stairs a man passed them heading in the opposite direction. He was carrying a bunch of flowers.

'Do you think that's him?' Fatima said.

'My mum'll be annoyed that I saw him before her. She always reckons that she has to give all Auntie Bex's boyfriends the once over before they meet the rest of the family. She says that Bex has no sense of taste.'

'He looked alright to me,' Fatima giggled. 'Anyway, his visit helped us. She might have been more cautious about telling us Phyllis Prince's address another time, but she was in a hurry.'

They joined the others and relayed the information they'd gained.

'What do we do now?' Lee asked. 'We can't just hang around waiting. Phyllis Prince would spot us. Do we just keep a secret watch on her? See who she meets and where she goes? Other stuff like that?'

Rowan spoke up. 'If you watch detective programmes on the telly, they have an information board that they stick bits of evidence on. Then they see what links together. We could do that. Who wants to be in charge of it?'

Danny said, 'Me. I like mind maps. My support teacher showed me how to do them on a computer. And Gramps isn't nosey. He won't ask me what I'm up to.'

Fatima was looking around at the untidy flower beds that surrounded the lawn. 'Lee and me could say to his auntie that we could help tidy the plants. You know, do some weeding and rake up the dead leaves. That way we'd be here for a good reason. Phyllis Prince wouldn't recognise us if we wore old clothes. Then, when we saw her go out, we could phone one of you and you could follow her. You'd have to be close by, though.'

They all agreed that this was a workable plan, though Kerry spotted one problem.

'What if your auntie chats to Phyllis Prince and asks her about the returned book that doesn't actually exist? It's a made-up story. She'll guess it was us.'

Fatima had another brainwave. 'Well, let's make it a true one. The hospital is just over there. It's got a charity stall selling second hand books. We'll get one, write her name in it and leave it outside her door. Then, if Lee's auntie does mention it, it will make sense.'

Josh said, 'You're a genius, Fatima!'

Kerry laughed. 'You said that about Fatima last week, Josh. Are you looking for a snog from her or something?'

Fatima and Josh both giggled with the rest of them, though they both looked totally embarrassed.

* * *

The plan worked well for the first part of the afternoon. Kerry and Rowan wheeled Wolfie across to the hospital where they bought a romance paperback. Rowan wrote the name *Phyllis Prince* on the first page as neatly as she could. Kerry found a piece of scrap notepaper on the counter, so she wrote a short message on it stating *we thought this might be yours*, which she slipped inside the cover. They returned to the others, and Lee took it across to the flats, leaving it outside the door to number three. Lee and Fatima stayed in order to pull a few weeds out of the flower beds while the rest of the gang left. Kerry and Rowan only went as far as the hospital, where they sat chatting on a low wall at the front. The others went down to the beach gardens to wait.

Things started to go wrong after an hour. The main door to the flats opened and the man who'd been visiting Lee's auntie came out, arm in arm with Bex herself. She took one look at Lee and Fatima and stopped dead.

'What on earth are you two doing here?' she gasped. Then, louder, 'What are you up to, Lee? Explain yourself right now!'

'Well, we saw the weeds . . .' he began.

'We're members of a garden tidying group,' Fatima added quickly. 'Trying to improve the look of the town.'

Auntie Bex narrowed her eyes. 'Don't talk twaddle. Are you spying on me? If your mum has put you up to this, Lee Gibson, she'll get a piece of my mind. How dare you hang around here poking your nose into my affairs!'

139

It was just at that point that Phyllis Prince came into view around the corner at the end of the road. Fatima grabbed Lee by the hand and pulled him away. They both ran in the opposite direction as fast as they could.

'Oh no,' Lee gasped. 'I'm gonna be in so much trouble. Mum and Auntie Bex are only just on speaking terms at the best of times.'

'Well, the one good thing is that Phyllis Prince didn't spot us. At least I don't think she did. Come on. Let's go and find the others. One of them might think of something. It might not be the disaster you think.'

The rest of the group were horrified to learn how the plan had gone so wrong but couldn't think of a neat way out of the problem Lee faced. In the end, he decided to head home and explain his side of the story to his mum before she heard any complaints from his Auntie Bex. Fatima said she'd come with him, as a sort of backup. A good move, as it transpired, because things went wrong from the start. Aunt Bex wasn't the kind of person to hold back on a good moan. Unbeknownst to Lee and Fatima, she'd already phoned her older sister and lodged her complaint. Lee was walking into a trap.

He opened the front door, walked into the hallway and beckoned Fatima inside. His mother must have heard the door squeaking because she came out of the kitchen like a shot, arms folded and glaring daggers at him.

'What have you been up to, Lee Gibson? Don't I have enough trouble with my sister without you stirring it up even more?'

She looked up and saw Fatima standing behind Lee. She frowned.

'Who's this?'

'Umm, she's my friend, Fatima. She was with me up at Auntie Bex's. Look Mum, it was a total accident.'

Fatima thought she should back Lee up. 'It really was, Mrs Gibson. We weren't trying to spy on Lee's Auntie Bex. Honestly. We'd just returned a book that we'd found to one of her neighbours, but she wasn't in. We left it outside her front door. We just hung around a bit longer to see if we could catch sight of her. It was all a misunderstanding.'

Lee's mum looked from one to the other.

'In that case what was this nonsense about being part of a garden tidying group? What's that all about?'

Fatima grimaced. 'That was my fault, Mrs Gibson. I just said the first thing that came into my head. It was stupid of me.'

'And then you both ran off, I understand. What were you really up to?'

'Nothing, Mum. We really did take a book back. The thing is, Auntie Bex came out with the man and the neighbour arrived back at the same time. And we had pulled out a few weeds. They were still in our hands. I just knew nothing we said would make sense, so we decided to run. It was a bit stupid. I was embarrassed.'

'I can believe that.' She looked again at Fatima and seemed to relax a little. 'I've looked out a little card for you to write, Lee. Put a short apology on it, sign it and post it this afternoon before the last post collection. Maybe things might settle down then. For goodness' sake, we've got a big family wedding coming up in two weeks and she'll be there. I was hoping to stay on Bex's good side until then. Now this. You know how paranoid she can get.'

She hauled a jacket off a nearby coat hook and put it on. 'My shift starts in an hour. I won't be back 'til late. There's a pizza in the fridge for your tea.' She made for the door, then turned. 'Nice to meet you, Fatima. Don't forget the card, Lee. It's on the kitchen table.'

With that she was gone.

'Phew,' Lee said. 'That could have been a lot worse. I'm glad you were here, Fatima. She kept her temper in check because of you.'

Fatima glanced at her watch. 'I'd better be going. I've got to pick Miran up from the neighbours and get some dinner ready for when Mum gets in from work. Listen, when this is all over, do you think it might give us a story for the school magazine?'

'Wow. That's a great idea. It'll be loads better than any of the other *What I Did in the Holidays* articles. We could work on it together.'

'But we can't write about what we're doing, not with the police investigating what happened to Daisy. We've found out a lot about local homeless people. It could be about that.'

'Yeah. I never realised how vulnerable they are. It's kind of scary.'

Fatima turned her dark eyes on Lee. 'That's because you all live safe protected lives here in this country. You think it's the same all around the world, but it isn't. Loads of people live in awful conditions and they're

142

always scared of thugs and soldiers. And the police. In lots of countries police are crooks themselves. They've got guns and they use them on anyone they feel like.'

Lee didn't know what to say. She was right, of course.

Chapter 23: Hospital

The group arrived at the local hospital the next morning. Fatima's mother had discovered what ward Daisy was in but warned them in advance that only three people would be allowed to visit her bedside, and that the visit would need to be a short one. Daisy was still recovering from major surgery and needed time to recuperate. Kerry, Fatima and Josh were chosen to visit Daisy's bedside when they all arrived at the hospital the next morning. The others stayed outside the ward, alongside a uniformed police officer who watched them warily. She was stationed there because of concern for Daisy's safety.

Daisy was sitting up in bed looking around her when they arrived at her small room. She saw them approaching and a puzzled expression crossed her face. The three teenagers felt equally puzzled for a few moments. What was different about her? Of course. It was her appearance. Her face was clean with skin that almost glowed. Kerry guessed that one of the nurses had rubbed soft moisturiser into her cheeks and forehead. In addition, her pale hair had been shampooed, brushed, and pushed back from her face. It was held in place behind her head by a mottled clip.

'Doesn't she look different?' Kerry whispered to the other two.

Daisy lifted a hand to give a weak wave as the three teenagers settled down into chairs at the bedside.

'How are you feeling?' Kerry asked.

'I'll live. I'm a bit o' a tough bird,' came the reply. 'Was it you wot found me and got an ambulance? Everything's a bit muddled in me head.'

'Yeah, it was us. Do you remember we got some soup for you when you were still in that doorway round the back of the community centre?'

Daisy shook her head. 'It's all sort of dim.'

Josh spoke up. 'What happened to you, Daisy? Who hurt you like this?'

She looked vague. 'I dunno. I can't remember nuffin'. It was all dark, so I didn't see much. Someone was just hitting me with a stick or summat. Really hard. The cops have asked me, but I couldn't tell em much.'

'How did you get out to Osmington, into your brother's place? 'Cos that's where we found you, in the pony shelter.'

'The cops asked me that, too, but I couldn't remember nuffin'. I sort of remember crawling away. It was just getting' light. But I bin finkin' about it, just last night. I fink I got to a builder's van. It was parked near. A sort of pick-up. I saw it was from Osmington. I climbed up and hid under a sack. 'S all I remember 'til I come to in the village. The builder's is just down the road from Roger's. I got out and tried his house but there were no one in. So I got in the pony shelter.'

'Where we found you,' Kerry said. 'We did a bit of detecting, Daisy, and guessed you might be there, in your brother's house.'

'Yeah, the cops said I got you lot to thank. I dunno what to say really. When I makes me first million, I'll give some to you lot. You deserves it.' Daisy gave a cackling laugh.

'Do you know why they beat you up?' Josh asked.

'Nah,' came the reply. 'But he were vicious. I thought it were curtains for me. There was a dog. It were a brute of a thing. If it had gone for me I'd be a goner for sure. Someone kept it back. It were slavering all over its chops.'

Kerry narrowed her eyes but said nothing. Fatima also made the connection, but she too chose to remain silent. They were both thinking the same thing: Gobbie, with the snarling beast that terrified Danny. Skipper.

Josh decided to change the subject. 'Have you been living rough for long?'

'Yeah, but not here. I was up Birmingham way for years. I was always on me own, like. Never liked being tied down. I got in with a rough crowd and I lost me way. Got kicked out of me home for not paying the rent. I lost me job. It was a right bugger, I'll tell you. Really hard. I comes from this area originally so I thought I'd try me luck down this way. I didn't come straight into the town though. I wanted to fit in slowly, bit by bit, so I kipped down in the woods for a few weeks back in the summer. I only come into the town when it started gettin' a bit colder.'

'Didn't your brother want to help you out?'

'I never told him I was 'ere. I was going to, but the time was never right. I felt kinda awkward about it. You know, 'cos of the state I was in. He's got his own family, kids an' all. You know? What could I bring 'em, apart from trouble? So I kept shtum about being 'ere. Then, after I got beaten up and I got out there to his place, there was no one there. They wuz all away on holiday or summat.' She paused. 'I thought I was done for. Out there, in that shed. I thought I was a gonner. I would have been if it weren't for you lot.'

Kerry squeezed her hand. 'What woods were you kipping down in, Daisy? When you first got here?'

'It were out west, along Fleet way.'

'Close to Chesil?'

'Thassit. The country's a bit wild out there, but it's only a coupl'a miles out of town. I didn't wanna come into town too quick, like. I didn't wanna put someone else's nose outa joint. I wanted to see how things were for beggin', like, before I started. It were alright in the woods. I kipped down in an empty barn that were half falling down. Well, it were empty apart from some boxes stacked at the back. And a bit of straw that I bedded down in.'

Fatima spoke. 'Did you tell the police this?'

'Nah, I don't think so. Everything was all fuzzy in me head, y'see. I only just remembered it. It ain't important, anyway, is it?'

'Probably not. Do you want me to tell that police woman out there so she can pass it on?'

'Yeah, okay. Gotta stay on the right side of the cops.'

Kerry grinned. 'Dead right there, Daisy. Don't I know it.'

They were interrupted by a nurse, ready to give Daisy her medication.

'I think that's long enough,' the nurse told them. 'She needs to rest now.'

The trio left Daisy's room and returned to the ward's waiting area to re-join the others. Lee was intrigued once he heard that Daisy had lived in an old barn in the woods. 'Isn't that where the Moonfleet story was based? You know, the one about the smugglers in the olden days?'

Most of the others looked blank.

'What, you haven't heard of Moonfleet? I thought every school in Dorset would have lessons on it. It's a great story and was only just along the coast a few miles.'

'I know about the posh hotel there,' Rowan said. 'My neighbour's one of the chefs. It's super luxurious, she says. I fancy a bit of pampering there sometime. You can get a really great massage and the food's won awards.'

'Does it do pizza?' Danny asked, and the rest of the group burst into fits of laughter.

'Is that a hint of what you want for lunch, Danny?' Rowan asked.

* * *

The group discussed what they should do over lunch. They all felt that a visit out to the woods at Fleet would be worthwhile, but some suggested that a delay until the next day would be a good idea.

'That will give us plenty of time. We'll have all day,' Wolfie said.

Josh checked the weather forecast on his phone and looked pensive.

"This good weather's coming to an end,' he said. 'Tomorrow should just about be okay, but Friday will be wet and windy. It'll be the same over the weekend.'

'So what you're saying is, if we don't check out the woods tomorrow, we might never manage it?' Rowan said. 'It's back to school next week.'

'Yeah. I've double checked with two other forecasts. They're all the same.'

Wolfie took out his phone to check, then called his Mum. He finally broke into a smile. 'She's free tomorrow morning,' he said. 'And she can use the wheelie wagon from her work.'

The others looked puzzled.

'It's a sort of small minibus with room for wheelchairs. She can fit me in and all of you lot as well. She can take us out there. It'll only take ten minutes. What d'you say?'

'Great. Let's do it,' Kerry replied.

'So that just leaves Phyllis Prince,' Lee said. 'Why don't we spend this afternoon doing a bit more investigating of what she's up to? We know where she lives now.'

Fatima frowned. 'Only if you're happy with it, Lee. We don't want to get you into any more trouble with your auntie or your mum.'

'Maybe it should be some of us my auntie wouldn't recognise.'

'She knows you and me. And Phyllis Prince might recognise most of us. Danny would be the best. Maybe with Rowan? Wolfie could act as our control centre, and stay hidden but close by, along with Josh and Kerry. Lee and me, we can stay down the hill a bit. As long as we've got our phones with us, we'll be okay.'

Chapter 24: Eavesdropping on the Enemy

Phyllis Prince came out of her block of flats soon after lunch. She glanced around but didn't see anything out of the ordinary. A woman carrying shopping bags. A man unloading stuff from a car. A boy and a girl walking a small dog. She felt safe. That pesky group of teenagers made her feel nervous with their constant meddling. She really needed reliable help and advice rather than having to rely on Shazza and Tommo. She couldn't ditch the two of them though. Shazza was Gobbie's daughter and Tommo was Shazza's boyfriend. Gobbie used them for all kinds of errands, delivering packages to people in Weymouth, Portland and nearby Dorchester.

I suppose they're the only people he can trust, apart from me, Phyllis thought. She sighed and started walking downhill towards the town centre. How did I ever get mixed up with Gobbie? She knew the answer, of course. She'd been his girlfriend when they were much younger, and he'd supplied her with as much booze and as many fags as she'd wanted, along with the occasional package of drugs. That's when she was really reliant on him, all those years ago. She'd ditched the drug habit, but still liked her free weekly supply of gin and cigarettes. He'd told her that all she needed to do to guarantee her regular supply was to run the occasional errand for him. But just look at what it had recently turned into. Bullying that scruffy dosser-woman and then trying the same with the gang of kids who'd come to her rescue. That was when it had started to go wrong. Gobbie thought they'd be easy to put off, but everything she'd tried had just made those youngsters more determined to find that old biddy. It didn't make sense. And why did Gobbie want the woman gone anyway? She wasn't really doing anyone any harm, dossing down in that doorway.

Phyllis wondered if the tramp had found something out or witnessed something that Gobbie wanted to be kept hidden. But she, Phyllis, felt nervous about trying to find out what it was. Gobbie scared her. He'd always been a bit wild, but he'd become even more of a bully as he got older. He'd even started to punch her if she tried to escape his clutches. He used to disappear at times, making her wonder if she could escape from him, but he'd always come back again and start lording it over her. Where did he go during those spells? He must have a lock-up or a shed somewhere. A place where he stored his stuff. But where could it be? Maybe Shazza knew. She was his daughter, after all. The trouble was, did she, Phyllis, really want to find out more about what Gobbie was up to? It was probably safer not to pry. The more you knew, the more danger you might be in!

Shazza was in her usual place, hanging around outside the amusement arcade, with a group of her friends.

'Whad'ya want?' she snarled as she saw Phyllis approach.

'I just wondered if that gang of kids've been hanging about. Have you seen 'em since last week? Your Dad wants me to sort them out but I ain't seen 'em.'

Shazza was scornful. 'Nah. Mebbe they got more scared than we thought. Good riddance to 'em.' She turned back to her friends with a sneer.

Phyllis should have been reassured by this news, but she wasn't. Shazza had always been the least observant person she knew. Once they'd been talking on the pavement in the town centre and there'd been a screech of brakes and a dull thud as a car had hit a lamppost, narrowly missing a nearby pedestrian. Shazza had just kept droning on about her latest boyfriend and how he liked really hot curries. When the police arrived and asked them if they'd witnessed the incident, Shazza looked blank and said, *wot incident*?

Phyllis spoke to Shazza again. 'Is your Dad around somewhere? I needs to see 'im.'

Shazza turned back to face her, clearly annoyed. 'I dunno, do I? He's prob'ly out at his shed in Fleet. But don't go there. He don't think I knows about it.'

Phyllis walked away, feeling irritated, but then stopped. Fleet? So that was where he must keep his secret stash. It would make sense. Only a few miles out of town yet such a lonely area. Maybe she could pay a visit tomorrow morning. She could 'borrow' her neighbour's car while he was away on holiday.

* * *

Danny had been standing close by, with his back to the group, but he'd managed to listen in to the whole conversation. That was the advantage of being small; people didn't really notice you. Added to which, Shazza only seemed able to talk at one volume – loud. He sidled across to Rowan, who was pretending to look in a shop window, and told her what had been said.

'Where's she gone now?' Rowan asked.

Danny turned around and spotted the familiar black coat crossing the street and entering a nearby supermarket.

'Tesco,' he replied.

'Let's get back to the others and tell them. It kinda fits, doesn't it, Danny? Daisy told us that she kipped down in an old barn in the woods near Fleet. Then we overhear Shazza telling Phyllis that's where Gobbie has a shed. You know what I'm thinking? What if it's the same place and she saw something illegal?'

'Yeah. We need to find out what's going on.'

It didn't take long to assemble the rest of the gang. They'd been following in small groups and could have got together quickly in an emergency. Danny told them what he'd overheard.

Josh spoke. 'Well, that's settled then. We'd planned to visit those woods anyway. It's even more important now.'

Chapter 25: The Way Through the Woods

As soon as they met Wolfie's mum, the other Misfits thought they could see where he got his cheeky, outgoing personality from, along with his fair hair and freckles. She chatted constantly and grinned a lot. She also swore vociferously at one car driver who caused her to brake sharply by cutting in too quickly after overtaking the Wheelie Wagon. Even Kerry was impressed at the range of swear words she used. She dropped them off at the footpath entrance and told Wolfie to phone her when the group were ready to be picked up at the end of the afternoon.

'I've got a morning of baking planned,' she said. 'It's therapeutic, and Wolfie's great at testing the results. He's honest about my cakes and tells me exactly what he thinks, no holds barred. Ha!'

She waved and drove off. Rowan commented to Wolfie about how much like his mum he was, but Wolfie surprised them all by telling them she was his step-mum, not his birth mother.

'Loads of people say that I look like her and act like her,' he said. 'But she's not my birth mum. I love her to bits though, and so does my dad. She's just so cheerful and funny.'

The path they followed headed west, into the woods. It was hard surfaced, so Wolfie had little trouble in his brand-new wheelchair, a motorised model. He spent the first five minutes of the walk experimenting with the controls, trying to do wheelies. The trees that lined the track were deciduous, mainly oak and ash according to Danny, who seemed to have an encyclopaedic knowledge of woodland life, and their leaves were starting to turn to their final late-autumn colours. The change to windier and wetter weather that was in the forecast would probably start the mass-drop that would leave the trees in their final winter form, though that would be several weeks ahead. On this particular afternoon the birds were still singing high up in the branches and they spotted several squirrels foraging for nuts and acorns.

'I used to come along here with my mum and dad when I was small,' Lee said. 'I always found a big stick and used it to whack ferns and bracken. My dad told me I must be in training to become a dragon-slayer. I believed him, as well!'

The others laughed. 'We all probably had weird ideas like that,' Rowan said. 'I always wanted to be a ballerina. And this was me when I was a small boy. My parents used to try to reason with me that I could be a ballet dancer but that boys couldn't be ballerinas. They stopped after a while because they could see how upset I got.'

'Do you go to ballet classes now?' Lee asked.

'Not ballet 'cos I'm just too big-framed, but I do go to dance classes. I just love it. I'm learning salsa at the mo. It's totally cool. It's so sexy.'

She stopped, did a few twirls and wiggled her bum. The others laughed and applauded.

Fatima was looking at Rowan anxiously. 'Rowan? Do you think I could start? I mean, join your dance classes? Would you mind? I don't want to intrude, and I'll go somewhere else if you want to keep your dancing separate, as something that's special to you alone. But I'd love to learn to dance properly. It's always been a dream of mine, ever since I was small in Syria.'

Rowan stopped, turned and gave Fatima a hug. 'It would be great. I'd love you to come. I feel a bit awkward there sometimes, wondering what people really think of me. But with you there, it wouldn't happen. I didn't realise, Fatima. I guess we're all a little bit in awe of you. You know, because you're so super-efficient and so in control of yourself. But we've all got to find a way of letting off steam, haven't we?'

The group continued to chatter amiably as they made their way through the woods. They were keeping their eyes open for the old hut that Daisy had talked about but, so far, there had been no sign of it. The trees were becoming more densely packed as they followed the track further west. In several spots the path surface became wet as dank water drained from high ground on one side or the other, even though there had been little rain for weeks. The birdsong seemed to fade, and the place was left in near-silence, with an eerie atmosphere cloaking the woods.

Josh pointed to the ground in front of them, another damp patch. 'Tyre tracks. They're faint but something's been along here.'

They could see a brighter area ahead, so hurried forward into a clearing, expecting to see the ruined barn that Daisy had described, but it wasn't there. Instead, the westbound track they were following came to a crossroads, with paths heading off north and south.

'Which way now?' Josh asked. 'Why don't we split up and explore them all? It can't be much further, can it?'

Rowan replied. 'Yeah. I can't see Daisy walking for ages through these woods. She said she found the old barn by accident. It's gotta be close.'

Fatima looked doubtful. 'I suppose we could split up, but only if we don't go too far. If we went for five minutes, then met back here, we could pick on the most likely one. That's if none of us actually find the barn. I think she'd have gone straight on here. The chances are it's along there.' She pointed straight ahead.

'That's the best path for Wolfie's wheelchair,' Kerry said. 'So Danny and me can go along there with Wolfie. Rowan, you go with Josh down the left path. That leaves Fatima and Lee going up that narrow one on the right. Okay? And meet back here in ten minutes. If any of us finds the place, phone the others. Okay?'

* * *

Josh didn't enjoy being in the woods. He hated the feeling of being enclosed or restricted, and these trees were just too big. They seemed to form a dense barrier on each side, though he knew that wasn't quite true. There was plenty of room to walk between them if the need were to arise. It was just when you looked in depth and realised that the trees just went on and on, only broken up by clumps of bracken. Even that was dying back, the fresh green colour of spring and early summer now replaced by a brittle brown. There was still moss everywhere, though. Great spongy outcrops of it. He only just stopped himself from shuddering.

'Don't you like the woods, Josh?' Rowan asked. 'Only, you haven't said much since we got dropped off back at the lay-by. And that's not like you.'

He shook his head. 'Not really. It's so quiet. And I keep thinking they're closing in on me. The trees, I mean. They're kind of spooky.'

'Maybe you suffer from some form of claustrophobia. Do you get the same feeling in other places?'

'Yeah, a bit.'

He didn't really want to talk about it. If truth be told, he was uneasy talking to Rowan. His own father, who he admired deeply, was very much a man's man. In his view, men and woman were almost different species, with entirely different ways of viewing the world. And Josh had never had any reason to question this view of the human race. But now, with Rowan among his group of closest friends, he was full of doubt and he hadn't had time to think things through. She made him feel slightly uneasy, because there were moments when she was still quite boyish. But then she'd suddenly switch to talking about girly things with Fatima and Kerry. It was almost as if she was some kind of in-betweenie, still finding her place in life.

Josh had talked to his parents about the other members of the group, but for some reason he'd held back on explaining Rowan's place in the group. He was uneasy about their possible reaction. It was strange, really. They'd never given him any sign that they were intolerant towards trans or gay people. So why did he feel the need to hold back? He was now worried that he had a problem, some mean-minded bit of prejudice tucked away deep in his mind, out of sight.

'Penny for your thoughts,' Rowan suddenly said. She was smiling at him.

'Sorry, I was daydreaming. My mum catches me doing it a lot and wags her finger at me.'

She laughed. 'I do too. I used to spend hours pretending I was a girl in my thoughts. Just to escape from the misery I was in.'

'Yeah. With me, it's thinking about the sea and sailing. I saw Ben Ainslie last year. He's my all-time hero. My dad says I could do competition sailing if I wanted. I dunno whether I'm good enough though. And I dunno if a black boy would get into the squad.'

Rowan stopped and frowned. 'Josh, you've gotta stop thinking like that. You can do anything you want if you put your mind to it. Don't let racist idiots get in your way. Just go for it, even if it's really hard.'

'Has it been hard for you?'

She nodded. 'Yeah. Loads of people telling me I was being stupid. Every time I mentioned it. But my mum and dad slowly came round. And they can see how happy I am now. I can't have any serious treatment 'til I'm eighteen, but that's okay 'cos I can at least live the way I want to be now.'

'You're very pretty.'

She giggled. 'Thanks, but if you say that again, I might think you fancy me. Sorry, Josh, but I already have my eye on someone I met last weekend.'

Josh was embarrassed. 'No, I didn't mean it that way, honest.'

He looked around him. They'd been walking for nearly five minutes and had seen no sign of a shed, ruined or otherwise. And the path was getting narrower.

'Maybe we should go back,' he said.

Just then, Rowan's phone rang, its sound startling them. She listened, a look of shock on her face. She didn't just start walking back, she ran. Josh was hard pushed to keep up.

'There's something wrong,' Rowan gasped. 'They're in trouble.'

Chapter 26: The Fight in the Barn

The side path that led uphill was shallow at first but soon became steep, winding up a wooded rise. It also became muddier, forcing Fatima and Lee to pick their way carefully between soggy-looking areas of ground.

Lee looked at the path ahead suspiciously. 'Do you really think Daisy would've come this way?'

Fatima shook her head. 'Not really but we need to check. Look. It gets drier just ahead.'

Her right foot slipped at that point and she ended up sitting in a muddy puddle. She swore. Lee managed to stifle a grin and held out a hand to his friend. She grabbed it and managed to haul herself to her feet without getting any muddier.

'I've got a cold wet bum now,' she said, trying to brush mud off her jeans.

Lee picked a handful of dried fern leaves from a nearby clump. 'Do you want me to have a go?'

'Why not? I bet it looks awful,' she answered, sounding angry. Lee gently brushed what he could from her stained jeans.

'I didn't know you swore,' he said. 'Doesn't it go against your religion?'

She looked at him through narrowed eyes. 'What? You mean you expect me to behave like a good Muslim girl should?' She snorted then tried to twist round and examine the stain, nearly causing her to fall again. 'Is that the worst of it off? I can't see.'

'Yeah. Once it's dried it'll be hardly noticeable. And sorry, I didn't know what I meant.'

Fatima was still angry, though Lee didn't feel that it was aimed directly at him. 'I'm like my mum. I lost any faith I had back in Syria. After our house was shelled and Dad and Liki were killed, an official from the local mosque came round and said that we should thank God for our lives, that we'd been saved. Mum kicked him out of the room we were in and told him never to come round again, him or any of his parasite colleagues. And that's how I've felt ever since. Religion is just a parasite on human society, feeding off people when they're at their lowest. It's all so false it's laughable. I mean, a paradise where young warriors go to after their death, filled with luscious virgins looking after their every whim. I suppose I'd be one of those luscious virgins. But you're only a virgin until you do it, then you're not one anymore. So where do they all come from? It's idiotic. And your Christianity is no better. Priests abusing children and having their crimes covered up. What about that strange bishop who spent his time corrupting teenage boys and then got helped by loads of people in authority hushing it all up? Religion stinks. I hate it. All of it. They're all evil really, peddling a load of lies.'

Lee didn't feel so strongly about it, but Fatima was clearly upset. He didn't want to prolong her sadness and anger so changed the subject. 'I can't see anything ahead. We could just go as far as the next rise. If there's nothing there we ought to turn back.'

Fatima's phone rang. She listened carefully to Rowan's voice. She sounded breathless. Was she running?

'Kerry and Danny are in trouble,' Fatima said. 'Rowan and Josh are going as fast as they can.'

She looked at a narrow side track, leading downhill through the trees and veering off at an angle from the path they'd used in the uphill direction.

'D'you think this might get us there quicker?'

'Let's give it a go,' Lee replied. 'It's worth a try.'

They started to run.

* * *

'Could this be it?' Wolfie asked, looking at the dilapidated, shed-like structure that lay to the left of the path, in a clearing.

'Looks like it,' Kerry replied.

She and Danny went in through a gap in the front wall where a door had probably once stood. It allowed light to stream into the otherwise gloomy interior. Much of the timber looked rotten, which explained the dank musty smell that filled the interior. Stains on the floor in several places showed where water would probably drip down from the rickety-looking roof during rainstorms. A small heap of straw lay in one corner, looking slightly scattered. It was spread in just the right shape for someone to sleep on, or in. Something on the straw caught Danny's eye and he walked across for a closer look. He picked up a grubby pair of pink knitted gloves.

 'They look a bit like the ones Daisy wore that first evening we saw her,' he said to Kerry, who had followed him.

About a dozen boxes were stacked against the far wall, though the light was poor at that end of the shed,

164

so it was hard to make out much detail from where they were standing. Just then Wolfie, left outside by the other two, finally managed to manoeuvre his wheelchair over the lip at the entrance. He whizzed across the hard floor, coming to an abrupt stop alongside the stack of plain cardboard boxes. They were all sealed, apart from one that lay by itself at the end of the row. He peered inside.

'Whoa,' he exclaimed. 'Look at this lot. Fags and booze. But the labels don't look right.'

The other two came across for a look.

'Phoney,' Kerry said. 'It's all junk. We probably need to let the cops know.'

They didn't get a chance. At that point a scruffy van drew up outside with a screech of brakes and a man got out, followed by a big dog. Danny backed away fearfully. Gobbie and the growling beast, Skipper. He looked in and spotted the trio of teenagers.

Kerry had her phone out and tried to run past the man in an attempt to get outside and summon help, but he quickly stepped sideways and landed a hard punch on her right side, knocking her over and winding her. Her phone fell out of her grasp.

'I'll teach you, Kerry Fenners,' the man sneered. 'You're gonna get a lesson you won't forget in a hurry.'

Wolfie tried to reach Kerry but Gobbie turned and kicked hard at the wheelchair. It flipped over on its side and Wolfie became tangled in his safety belt. The dog advanced on Danny, its growl getting louder at each step, and its lips pulled back in a fierce snarl.

Danny found himself being backed into a corner. He was terrified. It was as if his worst nightmare was coming true. He floundered backwards, nearly tripping over, and put his arms out to stop himself falling. His left arm touched something hanging from the wall. It was an old, rusty rake. It was now or never. Somehow, he found the courage to swing the rake around in front of himself as he moved forward a couple of steps. The dog stopped its advance but didn't move back. Its snarl got even louder.

Danny swung the wooden-handled rake extra fast, moved forward and hit Skipper on the nose. The dog turned and ran outside, howling in pain. Danny was spinning the rake even faster now. He quickly stepped sideways and caught Gobbie on the head. He fell and sprawled across the floor. Kerry managed to crawl to her phone and called Rowan. Meanwhile Danny righted the wheelchair so that Wolfie became mobile again. He accelerated directly into Gobbie who was just picking himself off the floor, knocking him back down.

Danny threw the rake to Kerry then ran outside to the van and hauled himself up to the open window. He reached inside and took the keys out of the ignition, then hurled them as hard as he could into nearby bushes. The dog was nowhere to be seen, thank goodness. He phoned the police then ran back inside to help the others. They were fighting a losing battle with Gobbie. Kerry might be tough and fearless, but the man was almost twice her size. She was trying hard to keep him at bay by swinging the rake at him, just as Danny had done, but Gobbie was backing her into a corner and trying to grab the rake. Once he managed that, it would be all over for her. Danny ran forward and hurled himself at Gobbie's legs, wrapping his arms around them and pulling backwards. Gobbie tripped over and sprawled across the floor. Danny jumped on his head. Kerry tried to pin his legs down while she looked frantically around her for something with which to restrain him. There was nothing.

'Wolfie. Do those straps come off the chair? We gotta tie him.'

Wolfie undid his safety belt and tried to disconnect the straps but it was a slow business. Gobbie had already managed to brush Danny off his head and was starting to kick out hard at Kerry, who was only managing to hang on to one leg. Things looked bleak. That was the scene that greeted Lee and Fatima as they chased in through the opening. They jumped on Gobbie's back and he went down again. Wolfie managed to get the strap detached from his wheelchair and tossed it across to Kerry.

And then Rowan and Josh arrived. With six teenagers sitting on his back even Gobbie gave up the struggle. Kerry, now bleeding badly from the nose, secured his legs together with the strap. They climbed off him. He tried to stand but fell over again.

'Skipper,' he roared. 'Skipper. C'mere. I needs you!'

All they could hear was a slight whimpering noise from outside.

'He's not gonna save you,' Kerry said. 'He's scared of Danny.' She turned and grinned at her younger brother. 'You saved the day, Danny. You're a hero.'

167

They heard the sound of another vehicle drawing up outside. Was it the police arriving already, only five minutes after being called? They looked up as a figure stood in the doorway, silhouetted against the bright light outside. It was Phyllis Prince. She turned and hurried back towards her car. Josh ran out and noted the car's registration but needn't have bothered. It took the woman several attempts to turn the car in the narrow track and, a few seconds after she finally started to drive away, she was brought to a juddering halt by a police car arriving along the drive, blue lights flashing. Phyllis turned off the engine and sat with her head in her hands.

Two uniformed officers climbed out of the car, adjusted their caps, and walked into the barn. The sergeant, a middle-aged woman, looked wearily at Kerry, still sitting on Gobbie's chest.

'Kerry Fenners. What have you got yourself into now?'

Kerry gave her a grin and a wave. 'Hi, Sergeant Rose. Is George gonna cook us sausage and chips again?'

The young constable who had followed behind, laughed. 'Only if you've earned it,' he said.

'You bet. Specially Danny.'

'I might manage it if it's a special occasion.'

'It's a deal. We'll be celebrating. It'll be all seven of us though. And Gramps.'

A look of horror appeared on the young constable's face.

The sergeant, Rose Simons, dissolved in laughter. 'George, the look on your face is priceless.'

As several more police vehicles arrived, the sergeant was able to start organising interviews, and examine the contents of the barn. She opened several more of the boxes, discovering even more counterfeit goods. Perfumes, watches and more bottles of booze. She turned round and stared at Gobbie.

'Who's been a naughty boy, then?'

Phyllis Prince had been watching from the entrance. 'It's nothin' to do with me,' she said. 'I'm not with anyone.'

Kerry was outraged. 'You liar, Phyllis Prince. You've been spying on us all week. And we saw you when Daisy was beaten up outside the community centre. You were there.'

Chapter 27: Sausage and Chips All Round

'It's ready. Come and get it!'

The call came from the kitchen of the community centre, where George, wearing a tall chef's hat and white apron, was busy with oven gloves, and Sergeant Rose was on standby with a stack of plates. Rae, the police detective, was the last in line, armed with salt, vinegar and ketchup. The gang members filed up and filled their plates.

'Beans and mushrooms too. Wow!' Lee said, surprise in his voice.

'George is in training,' the police sergeant said. 'He's under strict instructions from his girlfriend to learn how to cook. Though I don't think she'd be very impressed if he dished up sausage and chips every night. My guess is that she'd expect something a bit more gourmet.'

'Is she posh then, Rose?' Kerry asked, squirting a big dollop of ketchup on her plate.

'Well, she's posher than me. And that's all I'm saying. I've probably said too much already.'

George was scowling at her.

'C'mon, George. We're friends. You can tell us,' Kerry answered.

He sighed. 'Her name is Jade, and you and Danny have met her. She played sax in that concert that Danny was in.'

Kerry's eyes widened. 'Not that tall dark-haired girl? Wow! She was so cool. And she was really friendly. It was her who talked me into going to college. Isn't she at university now?'

George nodded but said nothing else. Kerry realised that Rae was trying hard not to laugh. Something was going on between the three police officers, but Kerry decided it would be wise not to pry.

There was easily enough food to feed the group-members, the three police officers and Gramps, who was once again on caretaker duties. They all sat at a single large table.

'It all worked out well, but you were lucky,' Rae said as they were all finishing off their food. 'It could have all gone seriously wrong in the barn. That Gobbie is a criminal thug and he's violent. You should have told me what you were planning. Or someone else in the local police.'

Kerry spoke up. 'Yeah, but Rae, we didn't know he was gonna arrive. We just thought we were looking for where Daisy used to kip down before she came into the town. That's all. Honest.'

Rae watched her carefully. 'Okay. I'll believe you on this occasion. But you need to be more careful in future and think what could go wrong. You agree, don't you, Rose?'

'Totally. See me? I always check everything out beforehand. I want to live to a ripe old age, and so does George.'

'What's going to happen to Daisy?' Fatima asked.

'She'll be out of hospital next week and I think we've found her a place in a hostel for a while. But what happens after that is up to her. If she can find a job and earn some money, then she'd probably be able to find a proper place to live. There's a local charity willing to help and I passed on her details to them. That's the best I can do.' Sergeant Rose shrugged her shoulders. 'We'll be pressing charges against the man you call Gobbie, both for the assault on Daisy and on you, Kerry. There's a squad looking into his smuggling operation, so it looks as though he'll end up with a stiff prison term. But your Phyllis Prince, well, the evidence is a bit weak, so she may well be let off with a caution.'

'What's happened to the dog?' Danny asked.

'It's with the local RSPCA. They'll try to find a good home for it. Maybe it'll calm down a bit with someone looking after it properly.'

Danny shook his head. 'I dunno. It's had two really nasty people as owners. They've trained it that way, to growl at people and scare them.'

'Well, we'll see. Maybe with the right owner it'll become a nicer dog.'

Danny turned to his grandpa. 'Could we try, Gramps? I'm not frightened of it any more, not after it ran away from me in the barn.'

Gramps couldn't help but show his surprise. 'Are you sure, Danny? If you're sure about it, we could give it a go for a couple of weeks and see if it settles. What's its name?'

'Skipper.'

'Well, if you really want to. But at the first sign of trouble, it goes back. Is that understood?'

Danny nodded his head vigorously. 'Thanks, Gramps. I promise to look after it. It's just that I was thinking. It

172

isn't really Skipper's fault it behaves like that. He's had two bad owners. I just wanna give him a chance.'

Sergeant Rose looked at him. 'Well done, Danny. I think everyone and everything deserves a second chance.'

After the washing up had been done, the three police officers left.

'Phew. I think we got away with that, didn't we?' Kerry said.

Everyone laughed.

'And the Misfits solved its first case. Three cheers for that!'

They made so much noise that Gramps put his hands over his ears. He had a big smile on his face, though.

The End

The Origins of the Misfits

This novel has its roots in the characters of Kerry and Danny Fenners. I created them in my seventh Detective Sophie Allen novel, Shadow Crimes, where they appear as the troubled offspring of a criminal thug and his alcoholic wife. Danny has Asperger's Syndrome and Kerry's behaviour is appalling, reflecting her gross unhappiness with her life.

What do you do when your dad's a crook, your mum's always drunk and your older sister makes a bit of extra cash at school by allowing boys to feel her breasts at a pound a go?

Thirteen-year-old Danny Fenners had spent countless hours pondering such questions, often lying awake late into the night. He just wished his family was normal, like the ones he saw on TV. In those normal families the parents were mostly happy and only had a few rows, meals were prepared in a proper kitchen and were eaten at normal times around a table, people talked to each other about things, instead of shouting and screaming abuse, doors were opened and closed quietly instead of being hurled open and slammed shut in a rage.

When I introduced them into the story, I had no idea how their lives would develop. I quickly grew to like them both, even Kerry with her sluttish, sometimes violent and abusive behaviour. The psychopathic killer Tonto Leary, original owner of the slavering dog

Skipper, firebombed their house, killing their parents. But this resulted in the two youngsters moving in with their beloved Gramps and their lives were transformed. By the end of that novel their lives had settled down. They appeared in the final scene, where Danny was playing his saxophone in a concert and Kerry was in the audience with their grandfather and several other influential characters, including Rae Gregson. The uniformed duo of Sergeant Rose Simons and Constable George Warrander also appear in that novel, particularly when Kerry and Danny are whisked away to a safe house. George cooks them sausage and chips; Rae is the overnight supervisor.

I didn't want that to be a farewell to the two teenagers. I felt they had potential, particularly Kerry with her no-nonsense, aggressive approach to life. I finished my next Sophie Allen novel (No. 8, Silent Crimes) and was looking for something different to plan before I started work on novel 9. How could I use Kerry and Danny, and continue their story? It occurred to me that they were both misfits, outside orthodox social roles. That's probably why I liked them so much. I often feel that I'm a social misfit because of my own long-standing gender issues, so the idea of creating a bunch of misfit teenagers who get together to help their local community seemed a good one.

Rae Gregson first appeared in the third Sophie Allen novel, Secret Crimes. She was newly appointed to Dorset's Violent Crime Unit as a detective constable, its most junior member. She has since been promoted to detective sergeant rank and has a close working relationship with her two senior officers. Rae is very socially aware, and she does everything she can to support young people from minority backgrounds. The two uniformed police officers, Sergeant Rose Simons and Constable George Warrander, who arrive at the old barn near the end of this story, were on duty on the night of the fire-bombing. They took Kerry and Danny to a safe house where George cooked them sausage and chips the next day.

Maybe young people have rather more acceptance of, and tolerance towards, minorities than their elders and so-called betters. I sincerely hope so. I think we should all try to understand the concerns and anxieties of minority groups. We are all humans after all. I fully support all efforts to secure full equality for all people. Black Lives Matter; Trans Rights Are Human Rights; these are more than mere slogans. They are watchwords that counter the view that, somehow, black lives and LGBT lives are somehow of less value than orthodox white folk. This is an evil concept. After all, there is only one race: the human race. All of its members are of equal worth, no matter the colour of their skin, their gender identity or their sexual orientation.

I've grown to love this group of well-meaning teenagers who call themselves the Misfits. I hope you come to love them too. More Misfits novels are in the pipeline.

Acknowledgements

I'd like to thank my sons and daughters-in-law for their continued support and encouragement: Stephen, Malcolm, David, Kate and Kat.

Chapter 26 is titled "The Way Through the Woods". This is the title of one of my favourite Inspector Morse novels and its choice as a chapter heading was no accident. Colin Dexter's Morse books have always been an inspiration.

Please Leave an Amazon Review
If you've enjoyed reading this novel, please consider leaving a review on Amazon. It will help! Despite what you may think, most novelists don't earn a lot of money. Good reviews encourage more people to buy, and this helps us to pay our bills!

You might also want to read the next Misfits story, The Missing Pilot.

Printed in Great Britain
by Amazon